The Witch-Woman

Books by James Branch Cabell

Biography of the Life of Manuel:

BEYOND LIFE • FIGURES OF EARTH • THE SILVER STALLION • THE
WITCH-WOMAN • DOMNEI • CHIVALRY • JURGEN • THE LINE
OF LOVE • THE HIGH PLACE • GALLANTRY • SOMETHING ABOUT
EVE • THE CERTAIN HOUR • THE CORDS OF VANITY • FROM THE HID-
DEN WAY • THE JEWEL MERCHANTS • THE RIVET IN GRANDFATHER'S
NECK • THE EAGLE'S SHADOW • THE CREAM OF THE JEST • THE
LINEAGE OF LICHFIELD • STRAWS AND PRAYER-BOOKS • TOWNSEND
OF LICHFIELD, SOME OF US, PREFACE TO THE PAST, &C.

The Nightmare Has Triplets:

SMIRT • SMITH • SMIRE

Heirs and Assigns:

HAMLET HAD AN UNCLE • THE KING WAS IN HIS COUNTING
HOUSE • THE FIRST GENTLEMAN OF AMERICA

It Happened in Florida:

THE ST. JOHNS (WITH A. J. HANNA) • THERE WERE TWO
PIRATES • I GO TO MY FATHER (IN PREPARATION)

Their Lives and Letters:

THESE RESTLESS HEADS • SPECIAL DELIVERY • LADIES AND GENTLE-
MEN • LET ME LIE

Genealogies:

BRANCHIANA • BRANCH OF ABINGDON • THE MAJORS AND THEIR
MARRIAGES

The Witch-Woman

A TRILOGY ABOUT HER

JAMES BRANCH CABELL

*"Everywhere is rumored thus the story of the witch-
woman, and of her ageless allure, and of her inevitable elusion at the last of all her lovers,
whether crowned or cassocked or
ink-stained, who are
but mortal."*

WILDSIDE PRESS: MMIII

Published by:
Wildside Press, LLC
P.O. Box 301
Holicong, PA 18928-0301 USA
www.wildsidepress.com

First Wildside edition: 2003

TABLE OF CONTENTS ❧

A NOTE AS TO ETTARRE

EACH of these stories concerns the third daughter of Dom Manuel of Poictesme and Dame Niafer, that Ettarre la Beale of whose birth and first amours something has been recorded in *The Silver Stallion*. For the rest, it is after the fashion of a prelude that this trilogy about her rehearses, in narrative form, upon a sharply limited scale, those three main themes which the Biography of the Life of Manuel develops, in a narrative form also, but with more ample leisure: for this trilogy relates how Ettarre the witch-woman (a personage about whom and about whose lovers, "whether crowned or cassocked or ink-stained," John Charteris has spoken a large deal in *Beyond Life*) was loved by a chivalrous king and by a gallant clergyman and by a poet.

Ettarre, it may be recalled, was the cause of the twelve-year warring (1263-75) between her brother Count Emmerick and her rejected lover, Maugis d'Aigremont, Donander of Évre's son; and it has been told likewise, in *The Silver Stallion*, how at the conclusion of this war Ettarre married, temporarily, Guiron des Roques. An account of her extra-legal, and indeed extra-mundane, relations with forever young, lean red-haired Horvendile is rendered in *The Cream of the Jest*; and is touched upon in the twenty-ninth chapter of *Jurgen*.

Well, but it was her excessive beauty, they say, which provoked the unfriendliness of the three Norns, those ageing ladies at no season pre-eminent for their beauty, or for their benevolence, either. At all events, it was through the Norns' decree that Ettarre was carried away from Poictesme, in 1286, by Sargatanet; and it was through an evasion of the Norns, as you may read in the first section of this trilogy, that Ettarre was fetched back to Earth, rather early in the spring of 1879, upon the feast day of St. Tiburtius and St. Valerius.

Here one encounters a point somewhat abstruse and a fact which has not been recognized by all students of the Biography of the Life of Manuel.—For you may note that, through Madoc's adroit use of punctuation, time, upon this unexampled occasion, returned to the year of grace 1294. All that which had taken place upon Earth between 1294 and 1879 thus had to be canceled; and everything which had happened since 1294 had to happen all over again. In brief, the entire Book of the Norns from the year 1294 onward had to be rewritten, inasmuch as no one of its authoresses had bothered to retain a copy of this juvenile production.

Now the Norns, in preparing this revamped version of Earth's history, which predetermined all happenings on this planet after 1294, adhered to their first version as nearly as they could recall it; but much slipped their memory; so that they introduced here and there a number of inaccuracies such as must necessarily result from the attempts of three literary ladies to reproduce a collaboration so exceedingly ancient that all three of them had virtually forgotten its nature and its purpose.

Nor was it possible for the Norns to recapture the more richly romantic vein in which they had written, so many thousands of æons earlier, at a season when, relatively speaking, they were mere chits, before the Solar System had been installed in the universe. That, in short, the Norns rather bungled the whole performance will be disputed by nobody who considers the depressing history of Earth and of Earth's people in this second version, the version which is still in use among misled learned persons, and which still begets pessimism, because of lean red-haired Madoc's meddlesomeness.

It therefore appeared far better, in preparing the Biography of the Life of Manuel, to adhere to the first version of the Book of the Norns, just as one found it, among the intended books of yet other authors, in the library of John Charteris. This task has been performed faithfully. It follows that the generally received history of Earth ever since the year 1294 does differ noticeably, here and there, from the authentic first history of Earth as this history is preserved in the Biography of the Life of Manuel; but there can be no serious disputing as to which version is the more handsome.

The sources of these three tales appear various somewhat widely. That the first of them is based upon the *Madoc et Ettarre* of Nicolas de Caen was duly acknowledged in an introductory note to The Music from Behind the Moon when this story was first delivered to the public; and the redaction was put into English during the opening months of 1926, in a form rather different from that which it now displays, for possible usage in one or another magazine.

There was then no thought of giving it an independent publication. But when, just at this time, Guy Holt decided to leave Robert M. McBride & Company in order to establish yet another publishing firm, it seemed that this brief romance might not ungracefully go to its writer's main "literary creditor" as an expression of good will toward Holt's new venture. The story therefore was recast into its present shape, being enlarged, as one recalls matters, from twenty-four chapters to thirty chapters; and a while later, upon 1 September 1926, in an edition limited to 3000 copies, and illustrated by Leon Underwood, The Music from Behind the Moon had the honor of being the first book published by the John Day Company.

The White Robe was completed in April 1928, and was brought out by McBride's, upon 23 November 1928, in a limited edition of 3290 copies, with illustrations by Robert E. Locher. A memorandum made at this time by the author of The White Robe states, with a painstaking particularity:

"I attempted in this story to render certain portions of the Life, or Legend, of Odo of Valnères—taking my material from the text (*tom. vi, S. Hoprigis opera omnia*) published by the Rev. Fathers of the College of St. Hoprig, at Aigremont, in 1885,—and to blend into these excerpts La Vrillière's brief account of the blessed Odo's relations with sinister Gui de Puysange (*De Puysange et son temps*, pp. 5-7). Very little, however, except Gui's actual name is derived from the latter source.

"The seventeenth century manuscript (codex 43f31 in the Vatican Library), of which the Rev. Fathers' printed form presents a well bowdlerized version, ascribes to the old lewd sorcerer no surname; nor does the cautious and unknown compiler of this manuscript, who was dealing with his contemporaries, let it be remembered, presume anywhere to mention the then powerful house of Puysange. La Vrillière, writing after the French Revolution, could afford to be bolder; and Black Odo's story profits by the event."

The Way of Ecben, which for chronological reasons has been listed as the second part of this trilogy, was finished in May 1929, and published in the October of the same year. For this story Charles Garnier may be considered the main authority, even if a few religious details were perhaps borrowed from the late Dr. P. T. M. Stewart's fine thesis upon the mythology of Rorn. At this distance in time, one cannot speak with certainty as to these points.

I must now turn, in speaking of The Way of Ecben, to speaking about myself.

My decision to make an English prose version of a narrative which already had been put into English verse sprang more or less directly from the discovery made in January 1929, when I came to preface *The Eagle's Shadow* for the Storisende edition of the Biography, that for some seventeen years I had avoided, quite unconsciously, the chivalrous attitude toward life as a main theme in my writing.

"Let us return," I said at this period, "to our first loves. I will paint me one more chevalier, such as was Adhelmar de Puysange and Fulke d'Arnaye and Ed-

11

ward Longshanks and Antoine Riczi, completely. Yes, and in dealing with the lovers of Ettarre I must try to summarize, just as an overture rehearses those melodies which are to be developed later, the Biography's three leading themes."

I said then: "The Music from Behind the Moon is about Ettarre and the poet Madoc—who may or who may not have been called Horvendile after the losing of his wife and his wealth and his wits, and (as is Bülg's theory) after a restoring of his youthfulness, upon Vraidex, by Miramon Lluagor. About that I am not certain; I have not ever known much about Horvendile except that in flesh-and-blood life he was called Felix Kennaston: but I do know that The White Robe deals with Ettarre and a Bishop of Valnères who was notably gallant. In logic, therefore, now that I reach the eve of my fiftieth birthday, and bleak time permits me to complete but one more fable about Ettarre, I will write as to Ettarre and that traditionary ninth monarch of Ecben who was, above all else, chivalrous."

And I said likewise: "Yes, it is fitting, inasmuch as the publishing of the Biography of the Life of Manuel began with a tale about Felix Kennaston and Margaret Hugonin, that I should now publish, as the last bit of the Biography which I shall ever publish, that how far more ancient tale which Felix Kennaston put into Spenserian verse, and which Margaret Hugonin caused to be printed, as *The King's Quest.*"

Moreover, this story had the advantage of suggesting, in itself, some of the many reasons for my decision that

12

after I had passed fifty there should be no more books about Poictesme or Lichfield, or about any more of the inheritors of Dom Manuel's life. The touch of time, about the effects of which you may read in The Way of Ecben, with a king as time's laughing-stock, does not spare writers either. The uncharitable may even assert that The Way of Ecben quite proves this fact; and indeed it is a privilege of which they have taken full benefit. In any case, now that the units of the long Biography of Dom Manuel's Life added up to a neat twenty, which was convenient to the laws of Poictesme, and now that with a yet more coercive arithmetic the years of its compiler's life were adding up to fifty, The Way of Ecben appeared to me a fable well suited to commemorate the end of my twenty-eight years' sport with the Biography of the Life of Manuel. I could thus speak, as its epilogue, through the lips of King Alfgar, at the conclusion of his own wilful doings:

"I have served that dream which I elected to be serving. It very well may be that I have lost honor and applause, and that I take destruction, through following after a dream which has in it no truth. Yet my dream was noble; and its nobility contents me."

So I did write The Way of Ecben: and we published it, with an uncanny precision, upon 25 October 1929, the day after the stock market had crashed, and that which we termed bewilderedly "the depression" had set in, and the robust gay literary era of the 'twenties had ended overnight, so to speak, with The Way of Ecben for an obituary notice.

Now as a trilogy *The Witch-Woman* occupies in the Biography its set place with fair competence, I make bold to believe. Nevertheless, it is not shaped as my thoughts first shaped it. I meant *The Witch-Woman* to be a series of ten stories which had been worked out more or less thoroughly; and all which stories (now that *Something About Eve*, after being for ten years in composition, had at last gone to the printers, in the June of 1927) one intended to write in good time for the complete series to be published as a book in the spring of 1930.

This scheme provided nearly three years in which to dispose of *The Witch-Woman*, a period which under the reign of common-sense would have sufficed amply. But I had reckoned without taking into account the fond toil which I, like the tricked Norns, would have to squander in rewriting my own rather long book, in the shape of the entire Biography, between the latter part of 1926 and the begining of 1930, for the Storisende edition.

At this point clearness begets a continuance in unfettered egotism. It was not planned, when we undertook the Storisende edition, that I should supply anything except a special preface and a signature for each volume; and a contribution thus limited ought to have satisfied everyone concerned. The trouble was that when I had started upon this revised version of the Biography I found that I could not rest content with occasional decorative touches. So I elected, instead, to rewrite each book, whether it were for the first or the second or the third evincement of futileness, from beginning to end.

Some of the eighteen volumes involved seemed, it is true, to require not quite so numerous alterations as did others, so that upon the whole I most thoroughly changed those of which I was then producing my fourth printed version; but every one of them did an untiring, and from any practical standpoint a quite profitless, desire for that continuous perfection such as no writer can ever attain compel me to rewrite during those very busy three years and odd months. This time-wasting, while profoundly enjoyable, left me enough leisure in which to complete, in the shape of any wholly new work, apart from my prefaces, only The White Robe and The Way of Ecben before I had come to be fifty.

Upon that uncheery date I had determined to end the Biography, for reasons which you may find listed in the note on *Townsend of Lichfield*; and in this way, because of my foible for rewriting prose passages which as they stood would not seriously have outraged the standards of what many persons unsmilingly term American literature, did *The Witch-Woman* abate from an imagined dizain into a concrete trilogy. *The Witch-Woman* thus became the sole known exception to the fixed law of Poictesme that all things shall go by tens forever.

It follows that, as a whole, *The Witch-Woman* must remain always in John Charteris' library along with the first version of the Book of the Norns and the intended, uncompleted masterworks of none knows how many hundreds of other authors. When I last visited Fairhaven the finished dizain stood between John Milton's *King Arthur of Britain* and Frances Newman's *History of Sophistication;* and upon this rather rueful occasion a brief peep into the pages of *The Witch-Woman* convinced me that in the not ever electrotyped parts of it were included the very finest and indeed the only faultless examples of my writing.

The intended series, I observed, composed a quite bulky volume, bound in gilt-stamped brown cloth. It was published by McBride's, and copyrighted in my name, as of 1930—"First Published, February, 1930." Its rhetoric displayed with profusion each of the seven auctorial virtues; it contained with a twin prodigality no misprints; and in brief, this unique copy of *The Witch-Woman* so much impressed me that I was at pains to jot down and to preserve its Table of Contents.

One admired, to begin with, a preface headed "Hail and Farewell, Ettarre!" in hardly anything resembling another expository paper which I have seen elsewhere under the same title. And the ten episodes which the book yet furthermore contained one found to be, in their intended order: The Music from Behind the Moon; The Thirty-first of February; The Furry Thing That Sang; The Lean Hands of Volmar; The Holy Man Who Washed; The Little Miracle of St. Lesbia; The White Robe; The Evasions of Ron; The Child Out of Fire; and The Way of Ecben.

This much alone I set down in my note-book. Then I regretfully put back the most beautiful and the most nearly faultless of my so many writings in its right place, between *King Arthur of Britain* (a truly sublime drama, so I hear, although I have never read it) and that unsurpassed, malign, mordant *History of Sophistication* which was dedicated to, of all persons, meek me.

This never finished dizain was to have followed through many centuries and a number of kingdoms the adventuring of Ettarre; and it would have told about ten human lovers of Ettarre who, howsoever differing in other respects, yet one and all committed the grave error of touching, and of striving to possess amorously, the flesh-and-blood body which at that time Ettarre was wearing. But in the final outcome my intended generously proportioned dizain has dwindled into this slender trilogy. I regret the outcome.

Yes, I regret in all sincerity that from my typewriters, alike from the Corona and the Oliver, have come, and may come, no more stories about Ettarre, who always since 1913, when I first encountered her in *The Cream of the Jest*, has been the most dear to me of Dom Manuel's daughters. My comfort is that there forever will be new stories about Ettarre, under one or another name, written by the young men who will get fame so long after my decaying generation has entered finally its decreed limbo.

All the young men everywhere that were poets have had their glimpse of the witch-woman's loveliness; they have heard a cadence or two of that troubling music which accompanies the passing of Ettarre; and they have made, and they will make forever, their brave and passionate stories about the witch-woman, so long as youth endures among mankind and April returns punctually into the fine world which young people inhabit.

But we who are not young any longer, and who must behold Ettarre and all other matters with the eyes which time has given us—and who, despite how many glowing memories, must yet find in her music, nowadays, no more than was found by gaunt Alfgar at his questing's end,—we may not dare to depend upon our memories, howsoever splendid and dear they may seem to us, for the piecing out of any more tales about Ettarre the witch-woman. We may well dare, as Alfgar dared, to preserve our faith in that which is beyond and above us: but we would wiseliest keep faith, even so, in silence as to that which our lean human senses deny nowadays. Our memories alone remain. We that have come to middle life may not any longer behold Ettarre with that clearness which is granted to our juniors: and this is an unpleasant fact, this is indeed in some sort a taunt, which must, today and for all time, obscurely discontent the living of every poet who has entered into his prosaic and over-quiet maturity, and who has discovered, quietly, that of the lad who followed after Ettarre memories alone remain, nowadays.

Even so, it has been recorded how all these maimed and discontented, time-baffled poets yet cry to the witch-woman:

"We would have nothing changed. That loveliness which we saw once and then lost forever, and that music which we heard and shall not ever hear again, were things more fine than is contentment. Hail and farewell, Ettarre!"

THE MUSIC FROM
BEHIND THE MOON

EPITOME OF A POET

*"Judge thou the lips of those that rose up against me,
and their devices against me all the day. Behold their
sitting down, and their rising up: I am their music."*

FOR

CARL VAN VECHTEN

Whatever hereinafter

he may like

PART ONE

OF MADOC IN HIS YOUTH

—De grâce, belle dame, si je puis vous demander ce que j'ai à cœur
de savoir, dites-moi pourquoi vous êtes assise ici toute seule?
— Je vais te le dire, mon pauvre Madoc, avec franchise.

THE TEXT FROM GENESIS 〜

*T*oꜱᴜᴄʜ as will to listen I plan here to tell the story of Madoc and some little part of the story of Ettarre.

Now this is a regrettably familiar tale. It may possibly have begun with Lamech, in the Book of Genesis, —who was, in any event, the first well-thought-of citizen upon known record to remark, "I have slain a young man to my hurt!" And poets tell us that many poets whose bodies had survived to middle age have repeated this glum observation, although probably not ever since then, when Lamech spoke without tact, to their co-partners alike in the homicide and in married life.

Moreover, this is a regrettably inconclusive tale, without any assured ending. Nor is there any assured prophesying, either, that the next thousand years or so will remedy that defect in this tale, because the story of Ettarre is not lightly to be ended by the death of any woman's body which for a while Ettarre has been wearing.

And, lastly, this is a regrettably true tale such as no correct-thinking person ought to regard seriously.

1. FOUR VIEWS OF A POET ❧

*L*ᴇᴀɴ red-haired Madoc was the youngest and the
least promising of the poets about the cultured court
of Netan, the High King of Marr and Kett. When it
was Madoc's turn to take out his bronze harp from its
bag of otter-skin, and to play at a banquet, he assisted
nobody's digestion. And, as the art-loving King would
put it, twisting half-fretfully at his long white beard,
what else was the lad there for?

The best-thought-of connoisseurs declared the songs of
Madoc to be essentially hollow and deficient in, as they
phrased it in their technical way, red blood: to which
verdict the wives and the sweethearts of these connoisseurs were only too apt to reply that, anyhow, the boy
was quite nice-looking. The unthinking women thus
confirmed the connoisseurs in their disapproval.

But the strangest matter of all, in a world where
poets warm themselves mainly by self-esteem, was that
not even to young Madoc did his songs appear miracu-
lous beyond any description.

To Madoc's hearing his songs ran confusedly; they
strained toward a melody which stayed forever uncap-
tured; and they seemed to him to be thin parodies of
an elvish music, not wholly of this earth, some part
of which he had heard very long ago and had half forgotten, but the whole of which music remained unheard
by any mortal ears.

2. THE WOMAN LIKE A MIST ?~

*N*ow, upon a May evening, when a plump amber-colored moon stayed as yet low behind the willows in the east, this same young Madoc bathed with an old ceremony. Thereafter he sat beside the fountain meditatively disposing of his allotted portion of thin wine and of two cheese sandwiches. A woman came to him, white-limbed and like a living mist in that twilight.

"Hail, friend!" said Madoc.

She replied, with hushed and very lovely laughter, "I am not your friend."

He said, "Well, peace be with you, in any event!"

She answered, "There is for you, poor Madoc, no more peace, now that I have come to you all the long way from behind the moon."

And then that woman did a queer thing, for she laid to her young breasts her hands, and from the flesh of her body she took out her red heart, and upon her heartstrings she made a music.

It was a strange and troubling music she made there in the twilight, and after that slender mistlike woman had ended her music-making, and had vanished as a white wave falters and is gone, then Madoc could not recall the theme or even one cadence of her music-making, nor could he put the skirling of it out of his mind. Moreover, there was upon him a loneliness and a hungering for what he could not name.

3. WHAT WISDOM ADVISED 𝕰

*T*HEREFORE Madoc comes to the dark and ivy-covered tower of Jonathas the Wise. And the lean and kindly man put forth his art. He burned, in a tall brazier, camphor and sulphur and white resin and incense and salt: he invoked the masters of the lightning and of volcanoes and of starlight; and he recited the prayer of the Salamanders.

Then Jonathas sighed, and he looked compassionately over his spectacles. "The person that troubles you, my poor Madoc, is Ettarre the witch-woman, whom Dom Manuel the Redeemer begot in Poictesme; and whom the Norns have ordained to live with Sargatanet, Lord of the Waste Beyond the Moon, until the 725 years of her poisonous music-making are ended."

Madoc said, "How may a struggling poet avoid the spells of this witch and of this wizard?"

Jonathas replied: "There is for a poet no defense against their malice, because their weapon is that song which is an all-consuming fire. Still, as one nail drives out the other, and as one fire consumes another fire, so something may be done against the destroying pair with this."

And thereupon, lean kindly Jonathas gave to young Madoc a very large quill pen fashioned out of a feather which had fallen from the black wings of Lucifer, the Father of All Lies.

4. ONE PATRIOT'S REWARD ❧

Wᵢₜₕ this pen Madoc began to write down his songs before he sang them: and the pen made for him a new kind of song.

Now the connoisseurs nodded approval. "The sentiment is wholesome, and, in these degenerate days, regrettably rare." King Netan clapped his hands, he laughed aloud, and he gave Madoc a greyhound, a white tunic worked with green embroidery, and seven chests of gold coin.

Thereafter Madoc lacked for no reward, and every week he had a lovelier lady for his love. At all the royal banquets he sang his new song, of how enviable were Netan's people in every heritage and in their sturdy racial qualities, and of how contemptible the other nations appeared in comparison: and everybody applauded his remarkable rightness.

But Madoc one day put aside his harp, he removed an amorous countess from about his neck, and he went alone out of Netan's shield-hung hall. All at that banquet were applauding Madoc; but through the shouting he could hear a skirling music which derided his patriotic perjuries: and Madoc knew that the fatherland he was praising showed as an unimportant pimple on the broad face of the world, and that its history, or the history of any other people, was but a very little parenthesis in Earth's history.

5. SOME VERY ANCIENT GAMES &

So MADOC fled from the cultured court of Netan, where the superb emotions of patriotism were denied him by that music which a pallid and pestiferous witch was devising in the Waste Beyond the Moon. He fled southward, into the fertile land of Marna.

In a green field, beneath a flowering apple tree, a young woman was playing at chess against a veiled opponent. His face could not be seen, but the gray hand with which he now moved a bishop had four talons like the claw of a vulture. The woman was clothed in blue: about her yellow hair she wore a circlet of silver inset with many turquoises, and about her wrists also were bands of silver, and in her face was the bright pride of youth.

At the sight of Madoc this woman arose, she smiled, and in a clear sweet voice she cried out the magic word of the south, saying, "Berith!"

The veiled man was not any longer there, but beyond the apple tree you saw a thin gray wolf running away very swiftly.

The lovely girl then told young Madoc that she was Ainath, the queen over all this country, and he told her that he was a wandering minstrel. Ainath in reply said she did not know much about music, but she knew what she liked, and among the things that she especially liked was the appearance of Madoc.

30

6. *LEADS TO A COFFIN* ॐ

NOR did Madoc dislike the appearance of Ainath. Nowhere in her appearance could he find any flaw: she was, indeed, so confident of her perfection that she hid from him no portion of her loveliness, and she refused to cheat him by leaving his knowledge superficial.

Her generosity and her fond loving ways led Madoc quite to overlook, if not entirely to condone, this queen's alliance with the Old Believers, when Madoc by-and-by had found out the nature of Ainath's veiled opponent and what game it was that Ainath played within reach of the fiend's talons.

Meanwhile with Madoc she played other games, night after night, inside the carved and intricately colored sarcophagus in which, when the time came, Queen Ainath must be laid away under the dark and fertile land of Marna; for it was the intent of this far-seeing queen to make of her coffin a hospitable place, and to endear it with memories of countless frolics and of much loving friendship, so that (when the time came) she might lie down in her last home without any feeling of strangeness about her being there yet again, or any unwelcome association of ideas.

Now it was Madoc who, for the while, assisted Ainath in this poetic wise plan, and with all the vigor which was in him he set lovingly to work to keep that coffin dear to her.

7. REWARD OF THE OPTIMIST ∂⌐

*N*ow also, for Queen Ainath, and for the shepherds who served Ainath, young Madoc wrote noble songs. It was not of any local patriotic prevarications that Madoc sang in the green fields of Marna, but of an optimism which was international and all-embracing.

"This is a fair world," sang Madoc, "very lovingly devised for human kind. Let us give praise for the excellence of this world, and—not exactly this morning, but tomorrow afternoon perhaps, or at any rate, next week—let us be doing exceedingly splendid things in this world wherein everything is ordered for the best when you come to consider matters properly."

The kindly shepherd people said, as they cuddled each other in pairs, "This Madoc is the king of poets, sweetheart, for he makes us see that, after all, this world is a pretty good sort of place."

But Madoc looked with dismay upon their smirking faces, which seemed to him, beneath their hawthorn garlands, as witless as were the faces of their sheep: and upon the face of Madoc there was no smirk. For all the while that he made his benevolent music he could hear another music, skirling: and this other music derided the wholesome optimism which was in the singing but not in the parched heart of Madoc, and this other music called him, resistlessly, toward his allotted doom.

PART TWO

OF MADOC IN THIS WORLD

Je t'ai secrètement accompagné partout, dans les luttes et dans les combats, sur les routes, dans les rues et partout: ma musique t'a préservé des atteintes et des agréments et des illusions du monde.

8. "THE BRAVEST ARE THE TENDEREST" ॐ

MADOC fled from the shepherd land and from the hospitable coffin of Queen Ainath, wherein optimism was denied him. Now he goes westerly, into the mountainous country of the Emperor Pandras, the third of that name.

There Madoc encountered a gleaming company of archers and spearmen with red lions blazoned upon their shields. Their Emperor rode before them, in red armor, mounted upon a roan stallion: and they went thus marching to make war against the people of Ethion, as was their annual custom.

"Our old traditions and our national honor must be preserved," declared the Emperor, "but, nevertheless, this year a war is rather inconvenient."

Then Madoc sang the newest song which he had made with his black pen. He sang very movingly of how many young men would be killed in the impending war, and of how this fact would be a source of considerable distress to their mothers.

The spearmen and the archers dropped each a tear from each eye: the Emperor himself was heard to clear his throat. "I have a mother," said one warrior.

His neighbor replied, "I have not; but I formerly had one, and the principle is the same."

The entire army agreed that the principle was excellent; a retreat was sounded; and war was deferred.

35

9. PHILANTHROPY PROSPERS ❧

T H E N Madoc made yet other songs for the war-loving people of the Emperor Pandras. He made fine stirring songs about philanthropy, and many simple chanteys such as workmen use at their labors.

The warriors turned from their belligerent raids, to the building of schoolhouses and hospitals and public drinking-fountains and domed temples for their three national deities. Laboring, these warriors sang the songs which Madoc had made, and his songs put a new vigor in them: their philanthropic endeavors went forward the more nimbly because of Madoc's noble and inspiring songs.

"Build," Madoc sang, "for the welfare of those who come hereafter! Create for them a fairer and more enlightened world! Build, as befits the children of the great Builder!"

But in a while he heard another music: he reflected how stupid were these perspiring and large-muscled persons who toiled for the welfare of a problematic and, it well might be, an unmeritorious posterity, for people who had done nothing whatever to place anybody under any least obligations: and his songs, which brought benevolence and vigor into the living of all other persons, appeared to Madoc rather silly now that again he had heard the skirling music of Ettarre the witch-woman.

10. *SPOILS OF THE VICTOR*

*B*UT the people of Ethion, after they had waited a reasonable while for their annual war to begin, lost patience before this disrespect for tradition, and bestirred themselves. They invaded the country of the Emperor Pandras. They were driven back and were slaughtered cosily, in their own homes, which were then destroyed.

"Our triumph is gratifying," said Pandras, after he had attended divine worship and had sent for Madoc. "Only, now that we have won this war, it seems right we should pay for it; now that we have laid waste the cities of Ethion, to rebuild them is our manifest duty: and in consequence I shall have to redouble, or perhaps it would be more simple merely to multiply by five, the taxes which are now being paid by my people."

"Yes, majesty," said Madoc, sighing somewhat.

"It follows, Madoc, that immediately after we have tried and hanged the surviving leaders of Ethion, we shall need a new song from you, as to the brotherhood of all mankind and as to the delight which a proper-minded person gets out of discomfort when it helps his enemies to live at ease, because otherwise my people may not enjoy paying five times as many taxes."

"I withdraw, sir, to complete this song," said Madoc, and after that, he withdrew, not merely from the presence of Pandras, but from out of the country of Pandras.

11. THE COMFORTABLE MUSIC ❧

*J*UST so did it fare with Madoc in many kingdoms. He wandered everywhither, writing noble songs with his black pen. He sang these songs before great notabilities, before the Soldan of Ethiopa under a purple awning worked with silver crescents, and before the Pope of Rome in a white marble room quite empty of all furnishing, and before the Old Man of the Mountains beside a fire in a grove of fir trees at midnight. Everywhere people of every estate delighted in Madoc's song-making, and they applauded the refining influence of his art.

Wheresoever Madoc sang, though it were in a thieves' kitchen or in the dark cell of a prison, his comforting music became a spur to the magnanimity of his hearers. They overflowed forthwith with altruism and kindliness and every manner of virtue which was not too immediately expensive: they loved their fellows, upon no provocation detectable by Madoc: and they exulted to be the favored children and the masterworks of Whoever happened to be their tribal god, in a universe especially designed for them and their immediate relatives to occupy.

And Madoc envied the amiable notions which he provoked but might not share. For always, when his music soared at its most potent, he heard the skirling of another nature of music, which was all a doubtfulness and a discontent.

12. PUZZLE OF ALL ARTISTS ❧

*Y*ET, as it seemed, no other person heard that skirling music. No other person willed to hear a music which doubtfulness and discontent made unexhilarating. They thronged, instead, to hear the sugared and the grandiose music which Madoc peddled, and which, like a drug, buoyed up its hearers with self-approval as concerned the present and with self-confidence as touched what was to come.

They listened, and they grinned complacently, who were—the kings and the archbishops and the barons and the plowmen alike,—each one of them already a skeleton and a grinning death's-head so very thinly veiled with flesh and hair. They grinned, while at the feet of each lay crouched the inescapable gloom of his shadow, to serve as an ever-present reminder of that darkness which would presently leap and devour him. Meanwhile they listened to the bedrugging music which Madoc peddled: and every heart made of red, moving dust, upon a brief vacation from the lawns and gutters of earth, was exulting.

It troubled Madoc whenever he heard any of his hearers talk exaltedly about the songs which Madoc made with his black quill, and it troubled Madoc that not any of the noble songs which he was making could ever wholly shut out from Madoc's ears the skirling music of Ettarre the witch-woman.

13. LEADS TO A LIZARD 🐦

*T*HEREFORE he went to Maya of the Fair Breasts, who controlled Wednesday. Before her at that instant stood an amber basin with green stones set about the rim of it. Inside this basin was the appearance of a shining lizard with very red, protuberant eyes which moved and glittered as the panting creature whispered to Dame Maya about that which was to come.

When Madoc came, the wise woman arose and put aside her cold, familiar counsellor. She went toward young Madoc with a light of wooing in her proud and sullen face. He found her exceedingly handsome, but he said nothing about this.

Instead, before her kindling gaze, he looked downward. Thus it was that he saw the lizard had put on the appearance of a tiny silver-colored pig. As Madoc looked, this pig became a little horse, and then a sheep, and after that an ox, drifting out of one dwarfed bright shaping into another shaping just as a cloud changes. But Madoc said nothing about this, either.

He said only, "Do you, who are all-wise, show me that way in which I may win to the accursed witch Ettarre, who has made empty my life, who permits no magnanimities to flourish in my parched heart, and who turns to mockery the noble songs that I write with the quill pen made of a feather from the wing of the Father of All Lies!"

40

14. HOW POETS MAY
REFORM ❧

D AME MAYA led him to a peaceful place where
every kind of domestic animal was dozing in her fine market-garden upon Mispec Moor. Sheep and asses and pigs
and oxen and draught-horses all rested comfortably in
this peaceful place. They had not any care in the world,
and no desires save those which food and sleeping satisfied.

The wise woman said, "Through a magic well known
to me, poor Madoc, you may become as one of these
who have been my husbands."

He asked, "Were these once men?"

Maya of the Fair Breasts answered him, reassuringly,
"Yes: all these quiet and useful creatures at one time
were mere poets, troubled as you are now troubled, and
all these have I saved from that music which is made by
the witch-woman, as presently I will save you."

Madoc cried out, "I do not ask for salvation, but for
vengeance!"

She said, "In vengeance there is neither ease nor
wisdom; but upon Mispec Moor are both."

Madoc replied, "Nevertheless, I prefer that you tell
me in what way I may come to the accursed witch, and
may make an end of her music and of her also."

The sullen wise woman answered, standing now more
near to him, "That way I will not ever tell you, because
I like too much your appearance."

41

15. RIGHT-THINKING
REMEDIED 🦢

THEN Madoc sang yet another of the songs which he had written with the quill from the wing of the Father of All Lies. He sang of how much good there is in even the very worst of us, and of that priceless spark of divinity which glows in every human breast and needs but properly to be fostered.

The well-nourished beasts that once had been poets arose forthwith, and each lurched clumsily about upon his hind legs. "Let us be worthy, yet, even yet, of that heritage which we have denied! Let us abandon this wicked market-garden wherein are only ease and gluttony, let us discomfort the world's ease everywhere with right-thinking and with every other high-minded kind of intrepid morality!"

So they babbled and floundered about Madoc, who all the while sang on exaltedly and thought what silly creatures seemed these bemired and madly aspiring overfed animals.

But Dame Maya winced to see her fair name as a competent wife thus imperiled, now that all her transfigured husbands were in revolt. She hastily told Madoc the way to the Waste Beyond the Moon: he ended his singing: and the domestic animals fell back contentedly into the incurious sloth and the fat ease of the wise woman's market-garden, out of which Madoc passed toward his allotted doom.

PART THREE

OF MADOC IN THE MOON

Le *chevalier Madoc lui dit: Vous voir est ce qui pouvait m'arriver de plus agréable, et je voudrais être avec vous jusqu'à la mort.*
— Cela *peut bien être, dit la jeune fille.*

16. LEADS TO THE MOON ঞ্চ

ALL that which Maya of the Fair Breasts had commanded Madoc performed, with his sword and a forked rod and a cup and a five-pointed talisman. This magic brought to him a monster shaped like a feathered lion, but eight and one-half times as large, and having the head and wings of a fighting-cock. Upon the breast of the hippogriffin grew red plumage; its back was of a dark blue color; and its wings were white.

Such was the gaily tinted steed upon which Madoc rode, along strange and unhealthy highways. The spirits of the air beset him: sylphs beckoned to this fine young fellow; Lilith, that very dreadful and delicious Bride of the Serpent, pursued him a great way, because she liked the appearance of Madoc. Nevertheless, he won unhurt to the pale mists and the naked desert space behind the moon.

Ettarre was at her accursed music: the gray place throbbed with it: it seemed the heartbeat of the universe, and the winds that moved between the stars were attuned to its doubtfulness and discontent.

"Turn, witch, and die!" cried Madoc furiously, as he came toward Ettarre with his sword drawn.

She made an end of her skirling music, she rose, and now for the first time he saw the face of Ettarre. Then Madoc knew it was not hatred which had drawn him to her.

17. MORE LUNAR HAPPENINGS ⤳

*H*E PUT her lips away from his lips. Madoc saw that the desert place was changed. About them now was a quiet-colored paradise: lilies abounded everywhere, and many climbing white roses also were lighted by the clear and tempered radiancy of early dawn. White rabbits were frisking to every side. Instead of that music which was all a doubtfulness and a discontent, you could now hear doves calling to their mates very softly.

"Love has wrought this lovely miracle," Ettarre remarked, without any sign of disapproval.

Madoc replied: "Love has brought beauty into this place. Now also shall my ever-living love bring liberty to you, and loose you from all bonds excepting only my embraces."

Ettarre answered: "I like your appearance: your embrace is strong and comforting: but there can be no liberty for me until the 725 years of my post-lunar music-making are ended. No man may alter any word of the Norns' decree: and they have decreed that for 725 years my master Sargatanet shall retain me here as his scholar and his prisoner."

Madoc said, jealously: "What else has this Sargatanet taught you save music? No, do you not tell me that, but do you tell me instead the way to your music-master, whom I intend to discharge."

18. TRUISMS COME HIGH ❧

*T*HEREAFTER hand in hand they passed toward Sargatanet where he sat under a vine which bore fruit of five different colors. Kneeling before the porphyry throne of Sargatanet at that instant were the five lords of hunger and fire and cold, of darkness and of madness. To each of these he was assigning the vexations to be completed during that week.

When his servants had departed earthward, to work the will of Sargatanet among mankind, and to stir up in human hearts the doubtfulness and the discontent which endlessly oppressed the heart of Sargatanet, then the gaunt master of the Waste Beyond the Moon bent down toward where Madoc and Ettarre stood at his ankle. He heard the plea of Madoc, and he heard the threats of Madoc, impartially; and Sargatanet shrugged his winged shoulders.

"That which is written by the Norns," said Sargatanet, "cannot be evaded. The Norns have written all Earth's history, they have recorded its Contents and its Colophon also. No man nor any god may alter any word of that which the Gray Three have written. For one, I would not grieve if such an evasion were possible, because Ettarre has now been my scholar and my prisoner for some 592 years. And you know what women are. That is why I do not bother to criticize seriously the writing of the three Norns."

19. THE NATURE OF WOMEN &

*T*HEN Madoc said: "I am not certain that I do know what women are; but I know their ways are pleasant. Their lips have been dear to me. They have yet other possessions in which I have taken delight. A woman is a riddle without any answer; she is not mere bed-furnishing; she is a rapture very brightly colored; she is a holiness which I am content to adore without under-standing: and among all women who keep breath in them Ettarre has not her equal.

"And besides," Madoc continued, "Ettarre is more durable than are other women; for she is more than 592 years old; and never in the moon would you sus-pect it. Hers and hers only, it has been remarked by the diffident voice of understatement, is that perfect beauty of which all young poets have had their fitful glimpses. Her beauty is ageless. Her beauty has in it no flaw. And so, even if the completeness of the beauty of Ettarre may demolish common-sense, yet a generous-minded person will be ready to condone its excesses. A generous-minded person will concede, without any cowardly beating about the bushes of reticence, that among all women who keep breath in them Ettarre has not her equal."

Sargatanet replied: "Do you please stop talking. For we know what poets are; and all we immortals know what women are. But we cannot do anything whatever about it."

20. *LOVE SCORES A POINT* ଓ

*T*HEN Sargatanet lifted the two lovers 592 feet, and through as many dead years, to the stone table beside his throne; and now before them lay open a book of which the pages were as tall as Sargatanet. This was the book in which the Norns had written the history of our world and all that has been upon Earth and all that will ever be.

"As I was saying," Sargatanet continued, "we know what women are. They very certainly do not excel as creative writers. Their imagination needs chastening; their bent is toward the excessively romantic. Thus the gray ladies have written a great deal of nonsense, and they have permitted entirely too much to hinge upon love affairs. Nevertheless, no man nor any god may alter any word of the Norns' out-of-date nonsense, of which all men and gods are a portion. So do these ladies keep the feminine privilege of the last word. And here it is written, plainly enough, that I shall retain Ettarre until the 725 years of her captivity are ended."

Madoc walked far up the page to inspect that entry in the giant book. "There is no need," said Madoc, "to alter any word."

With that, he took out the quill pen which had fallen from the wing of the Father of All Lies, he stooped, and with this pen Madoc inserted after the digit seven a decimal point.

21. *THE PEN OF THE CENSOR* ❧

*A*ND then of course—because whatsoever is written in the Book of the Norns must be fulfilled, and figures in particular cannot lie,—then a changing followed of all that which had been since seven years and three months after the beginning of Ettarre's captivity in the Waste Beyond the Moon.

Everything which had existed upon Earth during the last 584 years passed very swiftly and confusedly before the eyes of Madoc, as these things swirled backward into oblivion, now that none of these things had ever happened.

Twenty generations of mankind and all their blusterings upon land and sea went by young Madoc in the appearance of a sandstorm. Each grain of sand was a town or, it might be, an opulent and famous city, just as that city had been builded laboriously and painfully by some twenty generations of a people's cluttered, flustered, humdrum, troubleful, lumped hubbub, ungrudged because of that people's high dreams.

All the toil and glory and folly and faith and irrational happiness of the many millions whom Madoc's pen had put out of living had now not ever existed, because that which is written in the Book of the Norns must be fulfilled. And it was now written in this book that the bondage of Ettarre should endure for only seven and a quarter years.

22. NEAR YGGDRASILL &

N o т ever before had anybody essayed to cheat the Norns in quite this fashion: and so, from their quiet studio, by Yggdrasill, the Gray Three noticed this quaint expurgating of their work almost at once.

Verdandi, in fact, took off her reading glasses so as to observe just what was happening over yonder. "Oh, yes, I see!" she said comfortably. "It is only a poet altering the history of Earth."

Her sisters glanced up from their writing: and they all smiled. Urdhr remarked, "These poets! they are always trying to escape their allotted doom."

But Skuld looked rather pensively at each of the two other literary ladies before she said, "One almost pities them at times."

Then Urdhr laughed outright. "My darling, you waste sympathy in this sweet fashion because we also were poets when we wrote Earth's Epic. For myself, I grant we made a mistake to put any literary people in the book. Still, it is a mistake to which most beginners are prone: and that story, you must remember, was one of our first efforts. All inexperienced girls must necessarily write balderdash. So we put poets in that book, and death, and love, and common-sense, and I can hardly remember what other incredibilities."

With that, they all laughed again, to think of their art's crude beginnings.

23. THE CALL OF EARTH ❧

A POET is bold. There is no god in any current mythology who would have made bold to cheat the Norns," said Sargatanet, with odd quietness.

Madoc replied, "My pen is almighty; my pen is equally good at music-making and at arithmetic."

Sargatanet looked, for some while, with very pale blue eyes, at the two midgets down there beside his gold-sandaled feet. "Your pen makes music," Sargatanet then said, "such as all men delight in. Yet it cannot make my music. Your pen cannot write down nor may it cancel any line of the music which I eternally devise to be an eternal vexing to every poet, no matter what may be his boldness."

But, in the while that Sargatanet spoke such nonsense, Madoc had uplifted his Ettarre to the back of his hippogriffin. "I have done with all vexations!" Madoc cried out, as the glittering monster spread its huge white wings, and, flapping upward from behind the moon, plunged mightily toward Earth.

Thereafter the hippogriffin went as a comet goes, because its heart remembered that upon this Earth, among the dear hills of Noenhir, were its warm nest builded out of cedar trees and its loved mate brooding over her agate-colored eggs. And upon the monster's back, exulting Madoc also passed with a high heart, toward his allotted doom.

PART FOUR

OF MADOC IN THE OLD TIME

Ils vécurent ainsi pendant quelque temps: et la plume noire lui donna de l'argent, du bien, tout ce qu'il faut pour vivre heureux dans le monde. Ensuite le chevalier Madoc partit encore pour voyager.

24. THE OLD TIME
REITERATES &

*T*HUS it was that Madoc and his Ettarre returned to an Earth rejuvenated by Madoc's pen, and lived in the old time which long and long ago had perished before the time of Madoc.

Now the Northmen ruled as lords of Noenhir, where the hippogriffin had left its riders. These Northmen were an unsophisticated and hardy people, exceedingly brave and chaste, whose favorite recreations were drunkenness and song-making and piracy.

They welcomed the singer who could make such comfortable and uplifting songs as Madoc wrote with the quill which had fallen from the wing of the Father of All Lies. Madoc sang to them about their own importance, about the excellence of their daily habits, and about the splendid and luxurious future which was in store for their noble Nordic race: he made for them that music which incites mankind toward magnanimity.

Under their winged helmets the ruddy faces of the attendant pirates were aglow with altruism and kindliness and every manner of virtue. In their thorps and homesteads they welcomed Madoc, and paid him well. So Madoc builded at Noenhir a fine wooden hall: he and his Ettarre began housekeeping: and Madoc had not anything to trouble him, and his fair wife's embraces were now as dear to him as once had been the embraces of Ainath.

25. CONFECTIONER'S REPOSE ॐ

MADOC had not anything to trouble him. For many years he made his songs, and these songs made his hearers better and more happy. The only difference was that Madoc, now, had invested some little faith in his optimistic and uplifting songs; and much of what they said appeared to Madoc to be, quite possibly, almost true, here and there.

Madoc lived statelily, with all manner of comfort, in his broad hall, with dragons handsomely painted upon each end of it, and with a stout palisade of oak logs enclosing everything. The most prominent thieves and cutthroats in the country delighted to hear and to reward the singing of Madoc; Druids had crowned Madoc with the sacred mistletoe, as the king of skalds; the fame of Madoc was spread everywhither about the world: and the renowned poet had not anything to trouble him, and no heavier task confronted Madoc than to make praiseworthy music.

But Ettarre made no more music. "How was it that little air of yours used to run, my darling?" her illustrious husband would ask, very carelessly.

And Ettarre would reply, with the common-sense of a married woman: "How can I remember a music I never learned until centuries after this morning? And besides, what time have I for such fiddle-faddle with all these children on my hands?"

26. *WHAT WAS NOT*
TROUBLE ॐ

*M*ADOC knew that he had not anything to trouble
him. You were not really troubled by your vagrant notion that the face of Ainath or the face of Maya, or the
more terrible strange pallor of Queen Lilith's face,
seemed now and then to be regarding the well-thought-
of poet that was Madoc, with a commingling—for so
illogical are all day-dreams—of derision and of pity.

Nor could you call it a trouble that, now and then,
in such misleading reveries as were apt to visit idle persons when upon the plains and hills of Noenhir the frail
tints of spring were resting lightly, and ever so briefly,
the women whom tall, red-haired young Madoc had
thrust aside, because of the magic laid upon the prime
of his manhood, seemed to have been more dear and
more desirable than anybody could expect a mere boy
to appreciate.

Nor was it a trouble—rather, was it, when properly
regarded, a blessing—that the one woman whom you
had ever loved was endlessly wrangling nowadays over
your meals and the validity of your underclothing, and
over the faithlessness of all servants, and over the doings
of her somewhat tedious children; and was endowed,
nowadays, with the chronic and the never wholly smoth-
ered dissatisfaction which is the mark of a competent
housekeeper. Madoc very well knew that he had not anything to trouble him.

27 *TOO MUCH IS NOT ENOUGH* 🦢

MEANWHILE love's graduates lived with large ease and splendor. About their rheumatic knees were now the flaxen heads of grandchildren: they had broad farmlands, and thralls to do their bidding, and many cattle lowed in their barns. Life had given them all the good things which life is able to give. And Madoc had no desires save those which food and sleeping satisfied, and lean red-haired Madoc now was lean and gray and pompous, and unaccountably peevish also.

He rarely wrote new songs. But everywhere his elder songs had been made familiar, in all quarters of the world, by the best-thought-of pirates and sea rovers, as the sort of thing of which the decadent younger generation was incapable. Everybody everywhere was charmed by their resonant beguilement. Even the most callow poets admitted that with a little more frankness about sexual matters and the unfairness of social conditions the old fellow would have been passable.

Madoc, in brief, had not any care or need, nor, it was plain, any contentment. He fell more and more often to asking Ettarre if she could not recollect, just for the fun of the thing, a strain or two of the music from behind the moon with which she used to keep him without any home and miserable. And the old lady would tell him more and more pettishly that she had no patience whatever with his nonsense.

28. *THE RESPECTABLE GESTURE* ❧

*T*HEN his wife died. She died sedately, with the best medical and churchly aid, and after an appropriate leave-taking of her numerous family. There was a loneliness upon Madoc when he saw her white and shriveled old body,—so troublingly made strange by the forlorn aloofness of the dead,—lying upon the neat bed among four torches of pine wood. His loneliness closed over him like a cold flood.

He thought confusedly of the fierce loving which had been between them in their youth; and of their high adventuring because of a music which was not wholly of this earth; and of the ensuing so many years through which a sensible, unmoonstruck married couple had shared in all and in howsoever trivial matters loyally; and of how those fallen pale lips would not ever find fault with him any more. It was then that he fetched the black pen with which Madoc had written his world-famous songs; and he laid his pen in the cold hand of Ettarre.

"I call you all to witness," said Madoc, "that this day has robbed my living of its purpose and of every joy. I call you all to witness that I shall make no more songs now that I have lost my heart's arbiter and my art's arbitrary and most candid critic. Let my fame end with my happiness! Let the provokers of each perish in the one burning!"

29 *"THIS TRULY DOES NOT DIE"* 🦢

*T*HEREAFTER Madoc stood beside the funeral pyre. About him were his children and his grandchildren. A company of white-robed boys, from the temple of the local goddess of fertility, were singing what many persons held to be the very noblest of Madoc's many superb songs, the poet's great hymn about human immortality and about the glorious heritage of man that is the ever-living and beloved heir of Heaven.

Four bondwomen were killed, and their bodies were arranged gracefully about the pyre, along with the furnishings of Ettarre's toilet table and her cooking utensils and her sewing implements. Then fire was laid to all. Ettarre's frail aged body was burned so, with the black pen that was in her hand.

The white-robed boys sang very movingly; and they enumerated sweetly and comfortably, and exultantly, the joys into which this noble and most virtuous lady had entered yesterday afternoon. But old Madoc heard another music, unheard through all the years in which he had held Ettarre away from her lunar witcheries to be his bedfellow upon Earth: and the bereaved widower shocked everybody by laughing aloud, now that he heard once more the skirling music from behind the moon which, whether it stayed heard or unheard, was decreed to be the vexing of him who had cheated the Norns.

30. *LEADS TO CONTENT-*
MENT ࿐

S U C H was the end of his prosperity and honor, and such was the beginning of his happiness. Old Madoc went now as a vagabond, a trifle crazed, a trifle ragged, but utterly satisfied to follow after that music which none other heard.

Its maker fled always a little before him, inaccessibly: she held before her that with which she made her music, upon no cumbersome bronze harp but upon her heart-strings: her averted face he could not see, nor did he any longer wonder if it were Ettarre or some other who guided him. It was enough that Madoc followed after the music woven out of all doubtfulness and discontent which rang more true than any other music.

He followed its sweet skirling down the lanes and streets in which home-keeping persons chanted the famous songs of Madoc. Everywhere the smiling old wanderer could see his fellows living more happily and more worthily because of the contentedness and the exultant faith which was in these songs.

He was glad that he had made these songs, to be a cordial to guiltless men who had not cheated the Norns. Meanwhile—for him who had outwitted the Gray Three,—there stayed always yonder, always just ahead, another music, which was not wholly of this earth, and which a vagabond alone might be following after always, as was his allotted doom.

THE BEST POSSIBLE
POSTSCRIPT 🦢

*S*UCH is the story of Madoc: but of the story of Ettarre this is only a very little part. For her story is not lightly to be ended (so do the learned declare) by the death of any woman's body which for a while Ettarre has been wearing: nor is her music-making ended either (the young say), no matter to what ears time and conformity may have brought deafness.

I think we oldsters hardly need to debate the affair, with so many other matters to be discussed and put in order, now that all evenings draw in. If there be any music coming from behind the moon it echoes faintlier than does the crackling of the hearth-fire; it is drowned by the piping voices of our children. We—being human—may pause to listen now and then, half wistfully, it may be, for an unrememberable cadence which only the young hear: yet we whom time has made deaf to this music are not really discontent; and common decency forbids one to disturb the home circle (as that blundering Lamech did, you may remember) by crying out, "I have slain a young man to my hurt!"

EXPLICIT

THE
WAY OF ECBEN

A COMEDIETTA INVOLVING A GENTLEMAN

"I go the way of all the earth: be thou
strong therefore, and show thyself a man;
and keep the charge of thy god, to walk
in his way and preserve his testimonies."

FOR

ROBERT M. McBRIDE

*this brief and somewhat tragic tale, to commemorate
our long and rather comical association*

PROLOGUE AS TO THE
WARRING FOR ETTAINE ❧

*I*T IS an old tale which tells of the fighting between Alfgar, the King of Ecben, and Ulf, the King of Rorn. Their enmity took hold of them because they both desired that daughter of Thordis who was called Ettaine.

Two kings desired her because of all the women of this world Ettaine seemed the most beautiful. It was the blue of her eyes, that had the brightness of the spring sky when there is no cloud anywhere between heaven and the heads of men, which caused the armies of Rorn and of Ecben to meet like thunder clouds. Blood was spilled everywhere because of that red which was in the lips of Ettaine. The golden flaming of her hair burned down into black cinders the towns of Rorn and of Ecben.

Ulf's fort at Meivod, it is true, withstood all besiegers: but Druim fell, then Tarba. Achren also was taken: its fields were plowed up and planted with salt. Then Ulf captured Sorram, through undermining its walls. But Alfgar took Garian by storm, and he burned this city likewise, after carrying away from it a quantity of crossbows and tents and two wagonloads of silver.

There was thus no quietness anywhere in that part of the world, because of the comeliness of Ettaine. For two kings desired her: and her color and her shaping thus became a lofty moral issue, with a rich flowering of tumult and of increased taxes, and of corruption and of swift death everywhere, and of many very fine patriotic orations.

Then, in the fourth year of the fighting, the unexampled heroism and the superb ideals of the men of Ecben, which one half of these orations had talked about, were handsomely rewarded by the deafness of Cormac. This Cormac of the Twin Hills led a third of the armies of Rorn. He was paid the price of his deafness: for three maidens without any blemish in their bodies, and for four bags of blue turquoises, and for the silver which King Alfgar had captured at Garian, this Cormac became deaf to the other half of these orations, to that half of them which talked about the unexampled heroism and the superb ideals of the men of Rorn. He betrayed Rorn.

There was never a more gallant butchering than the patriots of Ecben then gave to the trapped patriots of Rorn under the elm-trees of the ravine at Strathgor. King Ulf alone was spared out of that ruined army where every other fighting-man lay in two halves, like the orations which had delighted everybody with sound principles in that part of the world.

So was it that the victory fell to Alfgar. None now withstood him. All that his heart desired he had, and he furthermore had all the forests and the cities and the sleek pastures of Rorn. Ulf, who was not any longer a king, prayed to his gods from out of a well guarded dungeon. And everywhere in Ecben, from green Pen Loegyr to the gaunt hills of Tagd, the barons and their attendants rode toward the King's house in Sorram, and all made ready for the marriage feast of Alfgar the high king and Ettaine the most fair of the women of this world.

1. OF ALFGAR IN HIS KINGDOM 🕊

*A*T THE King's house in Sorram was a hedged garden, with flagstones in the middle of it, about a little fountain. It was there that King Alfgar and Ettaine would sit and talk in the clear April weather.

"Ettaine of the blue eyes," King Alfgar used to say, "it is not right that your two eyes should be my mirrors. In each of them I find myself. A tiny image of me is set up in their brightness."

"Delight of both my eyes," Ettaine would reply to him, "in my heart also is that image set up."

King Alfgar said: "Ettaine of the red lips, it is not right that your lips should be making for me any music so dear. Some god will be peering out of heaven at my happiness, and a jealousy of me will be troubling that lonely god who has not any such fine music in his heaven."

"For no god and for no heaven whatever," the fair girl answered, "would I be leaving the Alfgar that has the pre-eminent name and is the darling of the women of Ecben. For in his strong arms is my only heaven."

Then Alfgar said: "Ettaine of the bright hair, it is not right that at tomorrow's noon an archbishop will be putting the crown of a queen of Ecben upon your shining head. Ecben is but a little land; and if the brightness of the crowns of Rome and of Byzantium, and of every other kingdom which retains a famousness, had all been

69

shaped into one crown for Ettaine to be wearing, the brightness of this hair would shame it."

Ettaine answered him, "It is not the crown which is dear to me, O heart of all my happiness, but the king alone."

"Why, but," said Alfgar, "two kings have loved Ettaine."

Whereupon the fond and radiant daughter of Thordis Bent-Neck laughed contentedly, and replied:

"Yet to my judgment and to my desires no person is kingly except Alfgar. And, as for that Ulf—!"

A shrug rounded off her exact opinion.

Such was the sort of nonsense which these youthful lovers talked upon the eve of their marriage feast, as they sat together in the hedged garden at Sorram, where the pale new grass grew raggedly between the brown flagstones, and the silver jetting of the little fountain wavered everywhither under the irresolute, frail winds of April. And around and above these lovers who were young the young leaves whispered in their merry prophesying of more happiness than a century of summers might ever ripen.

2. A DREAM SMITES HIM &

*N*o w it was in the night season of his marriage eve
that a dream came upon King Alfgar. Through his
dreaming a music went wandering. It was a far-off music
not very clearly heard, and a music which, he knew,
was not of this world. But that there was a sorcery in
this bitter music he knew also, for it held him motionless.

The champion that had slain many warriors lay upon
his couch, beneath a coverlet of lamb's wool dyed with
blue stripings, as still as a slain warrior. Upon him who
had all his desires came doubtfulness and discontent. He
desired that which this music desired, and which this
music quested after, skirlingly, and could not find in any
quarter of earth. For it was to the sound of this music,
as Alfgar knew, with a troubled heart, that Ettarre the
witch-woman passed down the years, and led men out
of the set ways of life.

So now a woman came to Alfgar where the King lay
upon his couch beneath the coverlet of lamb's wool, and
with this woman came a lean red-haired young man.
The woman smiled. The young man smiled also, but his
face became white and drawn when he had laid the
hand of this woman upon the hand of Alfgar, and when
the woman bent downward so that her face was near to
Alfgar's face.

She spoke then, putting her command upon Alfgar in
the while that he saw her face and the bright glitter of
her eyes and the slow moving of her lips. It was in this
way that Ettarre the witch-woman, whom a poet fetched

out of the gray Waste Beyond the Moon, to live upon our earth in many bodies, now put a memory and a desire and a summoning upon King Alfgar in the hour of his triumph.

Moreover, Alfgar now heard, very faintly, and as though from a far distance, a noise of grieving little voices which wailed confusedly. And that remoté thin wailing said,—

"All hail, Ettarre!"

Then one small voice was saying, "Because of you, we could be contented with no woman."

And yet another voice was saying, "Because of you, we got no pleasure from any melody that is of this world."

And still a third voice said, "Because of you, we fared among mankind as exiles."

Thereafter all these faint thin voices cried together, "All hail, Ettarre, who took from us contentment, and who led us out of the set ways of life!"

So was it that this dreaming ended. King Alfgar awoke alone in the first light of dawn, and knew that his doom was upon him.

3. THE SENDING OF THE SWALLOW 🦢

N o w h e r e in that part of the world was there any king more powerful than Alfgar. Young Alfgar sat upon his throne builded of apple-wood with rivets of copper, and his barons stood about him. Upon his fair high head he wore the holy crown of Ecben, the gift of Ecben's one god: the kingship over all Ecben was his who wore that crown. Gold rings hung in the ears of Alfgar; about the neck of Alfgar were five rings of gold, and over the broad shoulders of Alfgar was a purple robe edged with two strips of vair.

He bade them summon from the women's pleasant galleries Ettaine, the daughter of Thordis Bent-Neck, so that Ettaine might be crowned as Queen over Ecben. He bade them fetch from the dark prison that Ulf who was no longer a king.

Alfgar considered well these two who stood before him. Behind Ettaine were her bridesmaids. These maids were sweetly smiling tall girls, with yellow curling hair and clear blue eyes: each one of these four maids had over her white body a robe of green silk with a gold star upon the tip of each of her young breasts. But behind Ulf two of the masked men in red who had fetched him hither were laying out the implements of their profession, and the other two masked men were kindling a fire.

The barons of Ecben deferentially suggested such tortures as each baron, during the course of his military or juridical career, had found to be the most prolonged and

73

entertaining to watch. But the Archbishop of Ecben took
no part in these secular matters. Instead, he fetched a
chair of carved yew-wood, and he placed in it a purple
cushion sewed with gold threads, so that Ettaine might
observe the administration of justice in complete comfort.

Then, while all waited on the will of Alfgar, a swallow darted toward Ulf, and plucked from his defiant
dark head a hair, and the bird flew away with this hair
dangling from its broad short bill. At that, the barons
of Ecben cried out joyously. All were familiar with the
Sending of the Swallow: it was a Sending well known
to fame and to many honorable legends; for it was in
this way that the gods of Rorn were accustomed to put
ruin and downfall upon their cousins, the kings of Rorn.
So every baron now rejoiced to observe the morning's
appointed work thus freely endorsed in advance by the
approval of Heaven, now that Ulf's gods forsook him.

King Alfgar alone of that merry company kept silence.

Then Alfgar said: "This is the Swallow of Kogi. This
is a Sending of the three gods of Rorn. In what forgotten
hour did these three take their rule over Ecben?"

"Nevertheless, sire," remarked the Archbishop, "it is
well, and it is much wiser too, to preserve with the gods
of every country our diplomatic relations."

But Alfgar answered: "What the king wishes, the law
wills. And we of Ecben serve only one god, and one king,
and one lady in domnei."

Alfgar descended the red steps of his throne. He un-
clasped his robe of purple edged with a king's double

74

striping of vair, and he put this robe about the shoulders of another. Alfgar took from his fair head the holy crown of Ecben: the kingship over all Ecben was his who wore that crown which Alfgar now placed upon the head of another. Alfgar raised toward his lips the hands of Ettaine, he touched for the last time the lovely body of Ettaine, because of whose comeliness the heart of Alfgar had known no peace now for four years; and he placed her right hand in the right hand of another. Then Alfgar knelt, he placed his own hands between the hairy thighs of Ulf, he touched the huge virility of Ulf, and Alfgar swore his fealty and his service to the wearer of the holy crown of Ecben.

It was then that, after a moment of human surprise, Ulf spoke as became a king. But first he waved back the four masked men as they advanced to perform the duties of their office upon the body of Alfgar. The barons murmured a little at that, and the Archbishop of Ecben perforce shook his head in unwilling disapproval.

Nevertheless, Ulf pardoned the late treasonable practices of the fallen rebel now at his feet. Ulf cried a sparing of the thrice forfeited life of Alfgar, and Ulf cried, too, the King's sentence of eternal exile. Then Ulf said heavily,—

"And do you for the future, my man, go your witstricken ways in more salutary fear of the King of Rorn."

"And of Ecben also, sire," remarked the Archbishop.

Ulf said: "And of Ecben also! Moreover, do you go your ways, my man, in even livelier fear of the three gods of Rorn, who within this hour, and in this place, have defeated your wicked endeavors, and who by-and-by will be requiting your disrespectfulness toward their Sending."

The barons cried loyally, "What the king wishes, the law wills!"

But young Alfgar replied: "My king has spoken; and all kings, and all gods also, are honorable in their degree. Yet it is the way of Ecben to serve only one god, and one king, and one lady in domnei. And from that way I will never depart."

Thus speaking, he went into exile with not any person heeding him any longer. The people of Ecben had more important matters in hand.

For now was held the marriage feast of Ettaine, the most beautiful of all the women of this world, who upon that day rewarded handsomely the unexampled heroism and the superb ideals of those men of Rorn who had died because of her color and her shaping. She rewarded all these deceased patriots by crowning their beloved cause with victory, now that Ettaine became the wife of Ulf and the Queen over Rorn and Ecben.

And now likewise the altar of the god of Ecben had been overturned by Ulf's orders, and to the gods of Rorn was paid that reverence which they required. To Kuri the men of Ecben offered the proper portions of a shepherd boy and of a red he-goat, and in honor of Uwardowa they disposed of a white bull, and to Kogi they gave piecemeal a young virgin without any fault in her body or in her repute, in the old way that was pleasing to Kogi.

Thus generously did Ulf forgive that ruining which

had been sent against him in vain by the three gods of
Rorn, because, after all, as the King remarked, they
were his gods, and his cousins too. Nobody should look
to see unfailing tact displayed by one's cousins. And for
the rest, these gods would requite by-and-by, in an ap-
propriately painful fashion, the rashness of the misguided person who during that morning had interfered
with their divine Sending. Ulf, for his own part, pre-
ferred to leave that impious person to the discretionary
powers of an offended pantheon. Ulf desired only that—
within, of course, the proper limits, and in consonance
with the laws at large and with the various civic regula-
tions of Ecben,—the will of Heaven should be done in
every particular.

One need say no more (King Ulf continued) as to a
topic so distasteful. Secure in their heritage of noble
character and business ability and high moral standards,
blessed with a fertile soil and an abundance of natural
water-power, the patriots of Ecben would now press forward to put their shoulders to the plow and to free the
ship of state from the ashes and overwrought emotions
of war. The most liberal policies would be adopted by
a monarch whose one aim was to be regarded as the
servant of his people; immigration and the investment of
foreign capital would be encouraged in every suitable
manner; the cultural aspects of life would not be neg-
lected, but, rather, broadened to include interest in all
the arts and sciences and manufacturing enterprises generally. Taxes, for the present, and as a purely temporary
measure, would be quadrupled, now that the nation was
privileged to face this supreme hour, this hour wherein

to capitalize, for the benefit of oncoming ages, the united energy and integrity and resourcefulness of all Ecben, but not an hour, in the opinion of the speaker, wherein the fate of a misguided and disreputable exile was any longer a vital issue.

Thus spoke King Ulf from his tall throne builded of apple-wood with rivets of copper.

"His majesty," replied the barons of Ecben, "speaks as a king should; and we of Ecben are well rid of an unbeliever who has publicly offered any such affront to three most holy and excellent gods."

"In fact, the man's attitude toward religious matters was always dubious, whereas his morals were, alas, but too well known," remarked the late Archbishop of Ecben, as he hastily put on the goatskin robes of the High Priest of Kuri.

And Ettaine bent toward her husband fondly. All happiness adorned Ettaine: she was as fair and merry as sunlight upon the sea: each one of her beholders saw that Ettaine was the most beautiful of all the women of this world.

"Delight of both my eyes," said Queen Ettaine, "you speak as a king should. And, as for that Alfgar—!"

A shrug rounded off her exact opinion.

4. *"THE KING PAYS!"* ॐ

*I*T IS told that Alfgar fared alone to the dark wood of Darvan. This was an unwholesome place into which, of their own accord, entered few persons whose intentions were philanthropic: yet Alfgar journeyed toward Darvan now that the summoning of Ettarre had led him out of the set ways of life.

And it is told also that under the outermost trees of this forest sat a leper wrapped about with an old yellow robe so that his face might not be seen. Beside him, to the left side of this leper, was grazing a red he-goat.

This leper rang a little bell, and he cried out, "Hail, brother! and do you give me now my proper gift in a king's name."

"There are many kings," said Alfgar, "and the most of them are no very notable creatures. Yet in so far that a king is royal, a dream rules in his heart: so must each king of men serve one or another dream which is not known to lesser persons."

"Do you give me my asking, then," the leper replied, with a dryness suited to his more practical trend of thought, "in the name of Ulf, that is King over Rorn and Ecben. For my hands are frail; they are wasted with my disease: and I cannot do all the destroying I desire."

Alfgar said to this leper: "Ulf is but a little king, whom my cunning overthrew at Strathgor, and whom my pleasure raised up again in Sorram. Yet Ulf is royal, in that he would not forsake his gods, for all that they had forsaken him. Moreover, Ulf is my king now. And therefore I may not deny you."

So then the leper told his asking, and Alfgar seemed unpleased. But he smiled by-and-by; and, in that grave and lordly manner which merely rational persons found to be unendurable, young Alfgar said:

"To you that ask in my king's name I must give perforce your asking. For I will not depart from the old way of Ecben. And besides, my hands have touched the hands of Ettarre, and in the touch of sword-hilts and of sceptres and of money bags there is no longer any delight."

The leper then touched Alfgar's hands, and straightway they were frail and shriveled. They became as the hands of an aged person. They shook with palsy, and all strength was gone out of the hands which had made an end of many warriors in the noisy press of battle.

And yet another queer thing happened upon the edge of the wood of Darvan. It was that Ettaine and Ulf, and all the lords that yesterday had served King Alfgar, and all the houses and the towers of Tagd and Sorram and Pen Loegyr, and of every other town which was in Ecben, now passed by this unwholesome place in the seeming of brightly colored mists. And Alfgar wondered if these matters had ever been true matters, or if all the things which Alfgar had known in the days of his wealth and hardihood were only a part of some ancient dreaming.

But the leper put off his yellow robe, and in the likeness of a very old, lean man he pursued these mists, and he tore and scattered them with strong hands. So was it

Alfgar gave that which was asked in his king's name, and the fallen champion passed into the dark wood, and came near to the fires which burned in Darvan. They that dwelt there then swarmed about him, squeaking merrily,—

"The King pays!"

To every side you saw trapped kings in their torment, well lighted by the sputtering small fires of their torment, so that you saw each king was crowned and proud and silent. And to every side you saw the little people of Darvan inflicting all the democratic infamies which their malice could devise against these persons who had dared to be royal.

Alfgar went down beneath a smothering cluster of slender and hairy bodies, smelling of old urine, which leapt and cluttered everywhere about him, scrambling the one over another like playful rats. He could do nothing with the frail hands which the leper had given him, nor indeed could the might of any champion avail against the people of Darvan whenever once they had squeaked,—

"The King pays!"

Then the trapped kings cried out to Alfgar, with untroubled grave voices, and this is what the kings said in their torment:

"Have courage, brother! Our foes are little, but envy makes them very strong and without either fear or shame when they have scented that which is royal. There is no power upon earth which can withstand the little people of Darvan when once they have raised their hunting-cry, 'The King pays!' Have courage, brother!

81

for time delivers all kings of men into the power of the little people of Darvan. It is great agony which they put upon us, and from all that which is mortal in us they get their mirth, filthily. But do you have courage, brother, for to that dream which rules in our hearts they may not attain, nor may they vex that dream; even the nature of that dream evades them; they may not ever comprehend or defile that very small, pure gleam of majesty which has caused us to be otherwise than they are: and it is this knowledge which maddens the little people of Darvan. So do you have courage, as all we have courage!"

Meanwhile the little people of Darvan were getting their sport with Alfgar in disastrous ways. It is not possible for this tale to tell you about that which was done to him, for they were an ingenious race. Yet he came through the wood alive, because upon him was the mark of the witch-woman whose magic is more strong than is that magic of time which betrays all kings of men into the power of the little people of Darvan.

So he came through that wood yet living. But behind Alfgar those kings of men that were his peers remained secure in the dark paradise of envy, and the little people of Darvan attended to all their needs.

Such faithful service did this little people render very gladly to every king, because of envy: which, with not ever failing charity, endows the most weak with nimbleness and venom, as though, through the keen magic of envy, the sluggish, naked, and defenceless earthworm had become a quick serpent; and which is long-suffering in the while that, like a cunning sapper, it undermines the ways of the exalted; and which builds aspiringly, beyond the dreams of any mortal architect, its impressive temples of falsehood, very quaintly adorned with small gargoyles of unpleasant truths, and sees to it that the imposing structure is well lighted with malign wit and is kept comfortably heated with moral indignation; and which is a learned scholar that writes the biographies of the brave, and is openhanded to reward the faithful also with lewd epitaphs; and which, with stanch patience, follows after its prey more steadfastly than any hound pursues its prey; and which heartens the more flagrantly pious, alike in mosques and in chapels and in synagogues and in pagodas, with faith that all their betters are by very much their inferiors, if but the truth were known; and which is more eloquent than any angel to deride the truth; and which pleasantly seasons gossip; and which, with a consoling droll whisper, colors the misfortunes of our kindred and of our nearer intimates with agreeability; and which weaves, with a kinglike opulence, about all kings of men its luxuriant and gross mythology, of drunkenness and theft and lust; and which enlivens every human gathering so often as envy appears under some one of those lesser titles such as this monarch, perhaps over-modestly, affects when envy goes incognito among mankind as zeal or as candor or as a moral duty; and which yet retained in Darvan its dark paradise, wherein envy ruled without any check or concealment, and wherein the kings of men paid toll to the king of passions for every sort of high endeavor.

5. THE WAY OF WORSHIP ?

*N*o w at Clioth, near that cave which is dedicated to all gods, sat a leper wrapped in an old red robe which hid his face. Beside him, to the right-hand side of this leper, lay a large white bull chewing massively at its cud: and this leper rang a little bell when he saw that which the democracy of Darvan had left of King Alfgar.

"Hail, brother!" cried the leper: "and do you give me now my proper gift, in a god's name, before your many wounds have made an end of you."

"There are more gods set over man than I have hurts in my frail body," said Alfgar. "And it may be that no one of these gods is in all ways divine. Yet is each hallowed by the love of his worshippers: and in the hearts of his worshippers each god has kindled a small warming fire of faith and of enduring hope. For that reason should every god be held honorable in his degree."

"That may be true, inasmuch as it very certainly is implausible," the leper replied. "Nevertheless, you did not hold honorable the gods of Rorn. And, besides, I cry to you in the name of the god of Ecben."

"He is but a little god, a well-nigh forgotten god," said Alfgar. "I retain no longer any faith in him, and that hope which he kindled is dead a great while since. Yet this god also is made holy by the love of his worshippers, whom I too loved. This god who has gone out of my mind keeps, none the less, his shrine in my deep heart. So in his name I grant your asking."

"Do you give me, then," said the leper, "those golden rings which glitter in your ears."

"Very willingly," said Alfgar, for it seemed to him this was light toll.

But now the white bull lowed: and the leper nodded his veiled head as though in assent.

"—Only, now that I think of it," said the leper, "I must ask for a little more than those two gold rings. For my own ears, as you can observe, are not pierced: and unless I obtain pierced ears, then those rings will be of no use to me."

Alfgar saw that this was wholly logical; and yet this logic did not please him. Nevertheless, when the leper had told all his asking, Alfgar replied:

"I may not deny you that which is asked in the name of my own god, to whom I render every homage except the homage of belief; and I grant your asking. Moreover, I have heard the music of Ettarre, and I wish to keep in my memory the music of Ettarre, and I would not have it marred by my hearing any lesser noises."

So the leper touched the ears of Alfgar with strong hands, and the outcast King went down into the cave of Clioth. Then the leper rose, and put off his red robe, and in the likeness of a very old, lean man he went away to resume that labor which has not any ending.

And the tale says that in the cave of Clioth was not absolute darkness, but, instead, a dim blue glowing everywhere, as though the gleam of decay were intermingled here with the gleam of moonshine. Upon both sides of the cave showed a long row of crumbling altars;

and every altar was inscribed with the device of one or another god.

Thus upon the first altar that Alfgar came to was engraved: "I am the Well-doer. I only am the Lord of the two horns, the Governor of all living, and the Conqueror of every land."

But upon the next altar you read: "I am the Beneficent. I ordained created things from the beginning. There is no other god save me, who am the giver of winds to all nostrils, and the bestower of delight and ruin to every person."

The device upon an altar of square-hewn granite said: "I am that I am. I am a jealous god: my thoughts are tempests. Thou shalt have no other god before me."

Yet upon an altar of green malachite carved with four skulls was written: "I am the Warrior, the far-darting Slayer of all life and the Slayer of death also. No other god is my peer: through me the sun is risen, and I alone reign over the place where all roads meet."

Such were the devices upon these altars, and upon yet other altars showed yet other devices, but no living man might say to what gods any of these altars had been erected, for all these gods had passed down into Antan long ago. And about each of these altars yet knelt the ghosts of the dead, still worshipping where no god was, because in every age is born, to the troubling of that age, a man, or it may be two men, who will not forsake their gods.

So in that dim blue gleaming did Alfgar come to the ruined altar of the god of Ecben. He knelt there, among ghosts of all which once had been most dear to Alfgar.

Beside him knelt his sister Gudrun, who had died when they both were children. Hilda also was there, and young Gamelyn. Yonder knelt Alfgar's father—superb and slightly dull-witted, and more great-hearted than any person was nowadays,—punctiliously intent upon his religious duties, as became a properly reared monarch of the old school. And beside the father of Alfgar that long-dead queen who had been Alfgar's mother now turned toward her son that proud and tender gazing which he so well remembered.

But she did not remember. There was no recognition in the eyes of Alfgar's mother as she seemed to look beyond and through that Alfgar who was not any longer the King of Ecben, but only an aging vagabond upon whom was the mark of the witch-woman.

And a vague host of other persons whom he had known and loved, at Sorram and at Tagd, when Alfgar lived as a boy, knelt there in a blue gleaming. All these were wavering pale phantoms, and none of them was aware of Alfgar. These ghosts all gazed beyond and through him, as though he too were a ghost, in the while that they worshipped. Thus did they all keep faith, unthriftily, with that god who now had no gifts for his faithful, and who could aid them no longer, and whom no living person honored any more save only Alfgar, who knew that he knelt among the dead to honor a dead god.

"O little god of Ecben," Alfgar said, "it is right that I should bring to you an unthrifty giving of pity and of love and of all reverence. It is needful that I should not forsake you. It is very certain that in no quarter of this earth may I find any god whom I can serve true-heart-edly save you alone. For to the North reigns Odin; Zeus triumphs in the South; and Siva holds the East. To the West rule Kuri and Uwardowa, and Kogi also, who are Three in One. And the power of these gods is known, where your forever-ended power is not known any longer, and where your name is forgotten."

Then Alfgar made a lament, and this is what Alfgar said:

"It is known that Odin dwells in the North, at Glad-sheim, under a roof of silver, in a fair grove wherein the foliage of each tree is golden. All that which has been or will ever be is revealed to Odin, for this god has drunk, from out of a bronze kettle, the blood of a dwarf inter-mingled with rum and honey. Therefore does Odin govern all things, and the other gods of the North obey him as their father. He has nine and forty names, and under each name a nation prays to him. The power of Odin is very great.

"And it is known that Zeus holds Olympus in the South. He carries in his hand a thunderbolt, and an eagle attends him. The other gods of the South obey Wide-seeing Zeus as their father. The young women of the South obey him also, and he begets upon them heroes, but his heart is given to the boy Ganymede. Ganymede and yet other nimble, half-frightened boys obey this Zeus whose love fondles them. This Zeus is worshipped in the form of a ram because of his not ever tiring lusti-ness in all natures of love. In fornication, as in all other matters, the power of Zeus is very great.

"And it is known also that in the East three-headed

Siva has reared his dwelling place among broad shining pools of water in which grow red and blue and white lotus flowers. He rules there, seated upon a tiger's skin, upon a throne as glorious as is the midday sun. The other gods of the East obey this Siva as their father and their overlord. Whensoever it pleases him to do so, three-headed Siva descends from the brightness and the fragrance of his heaven to run howling about this earth in the appearance of a naked madman, besmeared with ashes and attended by starved demons and gray ghosts, for the power of Siva is very great.

"These things are known to all the pious that thrive in the North and in the South and in the East. My mind has knowledge of these things. My heart does not heed them."

Then Alfgar laid his shriveled hands upon the altar which was before him, and he bowed down his gray head so that it rested upon this ruined altar, in the while that Alfgar went on speaking his lament.

"For in the West, in my own West, it is known that the gods of Rorn have taken their rule over Ecben. From green Pen Loegyr to the gaunt hills of Tagd, where once a boy lived in fond sheltered happiness, the power of these three is supreme. Where once you reigned, O little god of Ecben, now these three reign, and they have honor. The burning of much incense blinds them; the men of Ecben bring to them red he-goats and white bulls and virgins; the needs of these three gods are duly served where your name is not remembered.

"These things are known. These things are known to every person, O little god of Ecben! But it is not known,

89

O very dear, dead Lord, in what hour and in what place the power went out of you, nor in what tomb you sleep discrowned and forgotten. O little god of Ecben, whom no other man remembers any longer, my pity and fond reverence, and my great love also, now go a-questing after you through the darkness of your unknown grave."

It was in this fashion that, in the faith-haunted cave of Clioth, Alfgar worshipped unthriftily the dead god of Ecben.

Now came toward Alfgar seven creatures having the appearance of jackals, save that each one of them wore spectacles. Such were they whose allotted work it was to discourage the worship of dead gods. Each raised a leg against the altar of the god of Ecben.

When they had finished with that task, these seven remarked, because of their sturdy common-sense:

"This man attempts to preserve the sentiments of Ecben without any of the belief which begot them. This man yet kneels before an altar which his own folly has dishonored, and he yet clings to that god in whom he retains no faith."

After that they carried Alfgar far deeper down into the cave of Clioth: and quietly, in entire darkness, they dealt with him as was their duty. But his life they spared, by howsoever little, and howsoever unwillingly, because upon this aging and frail wanderer they found the mark of the witch-woman whose magic is more strong than is that magic of time which overthrows the altar of every god.

6. THE LAST GIVING ౨෧

*N*o w at the farther end of the cave of Clioth you came again into gray daylight and to a leper who waited there in a black robe, which hid his face, but did not hide the glittering of the gold rings which hung in this leper's ears.

A flock of small birds arose from the dead grass about his feet, and flew away with many swirls and cheepings: you saw that they were swallows. A dark snake glided out from between his feet, and flickeringly passed down into the cave of Clioth, now that this leper rang a little bell.

"Hail, brother!" cried the leper; "and do you give me now my proper gift in a lady's name, before your feebleness and your wounds, and your great age also, have quite done with their thriving work."

"I once had more of ladies than I had of ills," replied Alfgar, "in the fine days when I was the darling of the women of Ecben, and no summoning had been put upon me. For in that far-off season it was I who summoned. I summoned with the frank gaze of a king who does not need to speak his desire: and out of hand a blush and a bridling answered me. So there was Cathra, and Olwen, and Guen, and Hrefna, and Astrid also; there was Lliach of the Bright Breast, and there was Una that was queen over the War Women of Mel; and there were yet others, before the coming of Ettaine. To each of these dear maids my heart was given at one time or another time: and in return they did not deny me their lips."

The leper spoke as if with doubtfulness, saying, "Nevertheless, it is better not to remain content with lip service."

"To many ladies of romance and of legend," Alfgar continued, now that his mind was upon this matter, "has my heart been given likewise; and those queens who ruled most notably in the world's youth have ruled also in my heart, because it is the way of Ecben to know that every woman is holy and more fine than a man may ever be—"

To that the leper answered, without any least doubtfulness, saying,—

"Stuff and nonsense!"

"—And moreover," Alfgar said, with the quiet pertinacity of an aged person, "it is the way of youth to desire that which cannot ever be attained."

"These reflections appear as handsome as they are irrelevant," the leper returned. "Now that you have done with your foolish talking, I cry to you for my proper gift, in the name of no harem, but in the name of Ettarre."

"And in that most dear name," said Alfgar, "I grant all askings."

So then the leper told his asking, and Alfgar sighed. Yet, in the grave and lordly manner of Alfgar, which merely rational persons found to be unendurable, decrepit Alfgar said:

"I will not depart from the old way of Ecben. Therefore I may not deny to anybody that which is asked in the name of my lady in domnei. And indeed, it may be that I shall make shift well enough, even so. For I have

92

seen the face of Ettarre, and I desire only to retain my loyal memories of that beauty which had in it not any flaw."

The leper replied, "Loyalty is a fine jewel; yet many that wear it die beggars."

When he said that, he touched the eyes of Alfgar, and Alfgar fared onward. But the leper arose, and put off his black robe, and from behind the rock upon which he had been sitting he took up the most sharp of scythes and the oldest of all hour glasses.

Then this very old, lean man cried out "Oho!" and yet again he cried "Oho!" and, after that, he went away chuckling, and this is what he was saying:

"I have well repaired the hurt honor of the gods of Rorn. I have well dealt with this Alfgar who, because of his fond notions, has yielded up to me willingly that which other men give perforce. For I take my toll from all. There is no youth which I do not lead into corruption; there is no loveliness but becomes my pillage; and man's magnanimity begets no bustlings which I do not make quiet by-and-by. I chill faith. I teach hope to deride itself. I parch charity. The strong cities, which withstand the battalions and the arbalests and the scaling ladders, may not withstand me. I play with kingdoms. Oho, but I play with every kingdom as I played with Atlantis and with Chaldea and with Carthage and with Troy. I break my playthings. I ignore neither the duke nor the plowman. All withers under my touch, and is not remembered any longer anywhere upon earth."

After that, the old man said:

"The earth itself I waste away into a cinder adrift in that wind which fans the flickering of the stars. I know this assuredly; for my skill is proved; and in heaven I keep always before me the cold, quiet moon as a model of what I mean to make of this earth. Oho, and in heaven also, all gods observe me with the alert eyes which rabbits turn toward the hound who is not yet upon their scent. They know that I alone exalt the Heavenly Ones, and that for some while I humor them, as I today have humored the vexed minds of the gods of Rorn. Yet these Heavenly Ones well know what in the end I shall make of their omnipotence. Let Kuri and Uwardowa, and Kogi also, have a care of my industry! The road behind me is littered with despoiled temples. The majesty of many gods is the dust in that roadway."

And this very old, lean man said likewise:

"But the road before me, oho, but the road before me, is obscure. Its goal is not known. If there be any power above me, it is not known. If there be any purpose anywhere in my all-ruining labor, it is not known. Yet if that power exists, and if that purpose and that goal have been set, I pray that these may end my endless laboring by-and-by, for I am old, and I tire of time's ruining, and there is no joy to be got out of my laboring."

7. OF ALFGAR IN THE
GRAYNESS🙡

*I*T IS told that infirm old Alfgar passed on a gray road beneath gray skies, and about him blew that wind which fans the flickering of the stars. The woman whom he met there was gray and fat as a fed coffin worm. She mumbled, between toothless gums,—

"Tarry! for I am that Cathra who was your first love."

And it is told also that the second woman he met was gray and lean. A piping voice came out of her lank quivering jaws, and that voice said,—

"Tarry! for I am Olwen whom you loved with your whole heart."

Then Hrefna, and Guen, and Lliach, and Astrid, and Una, and all the other most dear maids that Alfgar had followed after in his youth, cried out their willingness to reward his love. Ettaine came also, bent and infirm and gray; her withered hands trembled, and her guts rumbled rattlingly, in the while that Ettaine was saying,—

"Tarry, delight of both my eyes!"

For youth had gone out of these maidens; the years had pilfered their sweet colorings; and time had so nibbled away every part of their comeliness, that these were gray and decayed old harridans who leered and cackled and broke wind as each plucked at Alfgar's ragged sleeve in the windy grayness.

The gaunt tall King trudged onward.

But here, the gray way was littered to the right hand and to the left hand with a scattering of papers which flutteringly rose up in the persistent wind; and these also spoke with Alfgar.

"Tarry! for I am Oriana, the most faithful and most fair of all women," was the first thin whispering that the old King heard: "but Amadis is far from this place, so let us quickly take our glad fill of love."

Then another paper rustled: "I am Aude. Roland loved me until his death, and it was of Roland's death that I died; yet for your dear love's sake I live again."

And a third paper lisped: "I am Yseult, Mark's queen. But I loved a harper, and the music of this Tristram made all my life a music. Not even death might still that music, for our names endure as one song that answers to another song. Yet Alfgar now is my one love."

He saw then that upon these papers were very crudely drawn the figures of women, in old and faded colors; and he so knew that he was being wooed by the fairest ladies of romance and of legend. These swept about him futilely, adrift in the wind which fans the flickering of the stars: and all these paper figures were smutched with the thumb marks and the fly droppings and the dim grime of uncountable years. So did they pass as tatterings of soiled, splotched paper in which time had left no magic and no warmth and no beauty.

Alfgar sighed: but he went onward.

Then skeletons came crying out to Alfgar. And the first skeleton said:

"Tarry! for I am Cleopatra, I am that one Cleopatra

whose name yet lives. All the large world lay in this little hand, as my plaything. I ruled the South and the North. I ruled merrily, as befitted the daughter of Rā, the Lord of Crowns, and the well beloved of Amen-Rā, the Lord of the Throne of the Two Lands. The war drums and the shoutings of the legions under their tall crests of red horsehair could not prevail against the sweetness of my laughter: with one kiss I conquered Cæsar, and all his army. Then Antony brought me new kingdoms, and with each of these, and with him also, I played as I desired, at the price of another kiss. But my third lover was more wise and cold than were these Roman captains, and I died of his kissing, because that dusty-colored, horned worm was too fiercely enamored of my loveliness."

The gaunt tall King trudged onward.

And another skeleton cried out: "Nay, do you tarry instead with me. For I am that Magdalene whose body was as a well builded market-place from which men got all their desires. My love was very liberal: my love was a highway upon which glad armies marched in triumph: my love was a not ever ending festival where new guests come and go. Then a god passed, saying, 'Love ye one another.' But I stayed perverse, for after that time I loved him alone. In the hour of his tortured dying I did not leave him: when he returned from death I, and I only, awaited him, at the door of the gray tomb, at dawn, beneath the olive-trees, where the birds chattered with a surprising sweetness. But his voice was more sweet than theirs. Whithersoever he went, there I too must be: and for that reason he was followed by many who were enamored of my loveliness."

Alfgar sighed: but he went onward.

Then yet a third skeleton said: "It were far better that you should tarry with me. For I am Balkis; Sheba bore me, from out of the womb of an antelope; and in all the ways of love I was skilled. My skill was spoken of throughout the happy land between Negrân and Ocelis. King Scharabel chose me to be his queen because of that fine skill I had; and I rewarded him with a sharp troth-plighting. With one dagger thrust I took from him his kingdom and his life also. But it was in a bed builded of gold and carved with triangles that I conquered yet another king, when Solomon shaved from my legs three hairs, and I took away from him all his wisdom. So did he worship Eblis and Milcom after that midnight, because I served these gods very wantonly in their high places, and the lewd itching Jew was enamored of my loveliness."

But Alfgar put aside the lipless mouth, and all the other mouldering cold bones, of wise Balkis, also.

In such fashion did these skeletons, and yet other grinning small skeletons, flock after the tall wanderer and cry out to him. The sweetings of Greece and of Almayne and of Persia forgathered in that endless grayness with the proud whores of the Merovingians and of the Pharaohs, and each of these luxurious women wooed Alfgar. The empresses of Rome and of Byzantium came likewise: the czarinas of Muscovy and the sultanas of Arabia attended him. The head-wives of the Caziques and of the Incas, the nieces of the Popes, and the maharanees of the Great Khans, all flocked about

King Alfgar: and all were mouldy bones, in their torn and rotted gravecloths. Then from the mire along the gray roadway arose the voices of the queens of Assyria and of Babylon, who now were scattered dust and horse dung. All these, whom time had done with, now cried out wooingly to Alfgar.

But infirm old Alfgar went onward without heeding any of them, for so strong was the magic which Ettarre had put upon him that all these who once had been the fairest of the women of this world no longer seemed desirable. He came thus, in the grayness, toward a garden.

At the gate of this garden, beside the lingham post which stood there in eternal erection, sat a young man who was diverting himself by whittling, with a small green-handled knife, a bit of cedar-wood into the quaint shaping which that post had. His hair was darkly red: and now, as he regarded Alfgar with brown and wide-set eyes, the face of this tall boy was humorously grave, and he nodded now, as the complacent artist nods who looks upon his advancing work and finds all to be near his wishes.

"Time has indeed laid hold of you with both hands," said this youngster, "and the touch of time does more than the club of Hercules. It is not the Alfgar who had the pre-eminent name that I am seeing, but only a frail and half-blinded and deaf vagabond."

"Nevertheless," said Alfgar, and even now he spoke in that grave and lordly manner which when Alfgar spoke from a throne had annoyed the more human of his hearers, "nevertheless, I have not departed from the old way of Ecben."

"I know that way," the boy replied. "It is a pretty notion to have but one king and one god and, above both of them, one lady. Oh, yes, it is a most diverting notion, and a very potent drug, to believe that these three are holy and all-important. I too have got diversion from that notion, in my day."

The boy shook his red curls; and he said, shruggingly:

"But no toy lasts forever. And out of that notion also time has taken the old nobleness and the fine strength."

Then Alfgar asked, "But what do you do here who wait in this gray place like a sentinel?"

The boy replied: "I do that which I do in every place. Here also, at the gateway of that garden into which time has not yet entered, I fight with time my ever-losing battle, because to do that diverts me."

He smiled: but Alfgar did not smile.

"To be seeking always for diversion, sir," said Alfgar, with a king's frankness, "is an ignoble way of living."

"Ah, but then," the boy answered him, "I fight against the gluttony of time with so many very amusing weapons,—with gestures and with three attitudes and with charming phrases; with tears, and with tinsel, and with sugar-coated pills, and with platitudes slightly regilded. Yes, and I fight him also with little mirrors wherein gleam confusedly the corruptions of lust, and ruddy loyalty, and a bit of moonshine, and the pure diamond of the heart's desire, and the opal cloudings of human compromise: but, above all, I fight that ravening dotard with the strength of my own folly."

100

"I do not understand these foolish sayings," Alfgar returned. "Yet I take you to be that Horvendile who is the eternal playfellow of my lady in domnei—"

"But I," the boy answered, "I take it that I must be the eternal playfellow of time. For piety and common-sense and death are rightfully time's toys: and it is with these three that I divert myself."

Alfgar said: "Your talking is a piddling way of talking. I must tell you frankly, Messire Horvendile, for your own good, that such frivolousness is unbecoming in an immortal."

The boy laughed, without any mirth, at this old vagabond's old notions. "Then I must tell you," said Horvendile, "that my immortality has sharp restrictions. For it is at a price that I pass down the years, as yet, in eternal union with the witch-woman whose magic stays—as yet—more strong than is the magic of time. The price is that I only of her lovers may not ever hope to win Ettarre. This merely is permitted me: that I may touch the hand of Ettarre in the moment that I lay that hand in the hand of her most recent, foredoomed lover. I give, who may not ever take."

But Horvendile laughed at that, too, still without any gaiety. He then added:

"So do I purchase an eternally unfed desire against which time as yet remains powerless."

"But I, sir, go to take my desires, as becomes an honest chevalier," said Alfgar, very resolutely, as the infirm old King now passed beyond this fribbling and insane immortal.

The boy replied to him: "That well may be. Yet

101

how does that matter, either,—by-and-by—in a world wherein the saga of every man leads to the same Explicit?"

But Horvendile got no answer to this question, at this season, nor at any other season. So by-and-by he gave to this question a fine place among those other platitudes which he had regilded slightly in the while that Horvendile waited in the grayness, and about him was moving the persistent wind which fans the flickering of the stars.

And infirm old Alfgar went onward, beyond the lingham post, into the garden which is between dawn and sunrise.

8. HOW THE KING TRIUMPHED 🐦

IT IS told that all loveliness endured in this garden
whereinto time had not yet entered. It is told that,
advancing wearily through the first glow of dawn,
Alfgar now passed into the spring of a year which was
not registered upon any almanac. Here youth, as always,
lived for the passing moment: the difference here was
that the moment did not pass. And it is told also that
this ever-abiding moment was that moment wherein
the spring dawn promises a day more fair than any
day may ever be, and when the young leaves whisper
in their merry prophesying of more happiness than a
century of summers might ever ripen.

But Alfgar was no longer in the prime of his youth.
To every side of him, through the first glow of dawn,
young persons walked in couples, and they were glad
because they knew that the world was their plaything,
and that their love was a wholly unexampled love
which the dark daughters of Dvalinn, even those three
Norns who weave the fate of all the living, regarded
respectfully; and which the oncoming years all labored
to reward with never-ending famousness and contentment. These high-hearted amorists, who were young,
knew that time was a bearer of resplendent gifts; they
knew that their love was eternal; they knew also that
they were far more remarkable and more glorious than
any other pair of lovers who had ever existed: and, as

103

they walked there in couples, they mentioned all these facts.

But Alfgar walked alone: and of necessity, he looked at these youngsters with the eyes which time had given him; and it was with the ears which time had given him that he heard these chattering, moonstruck, gangling young half-wits talk their nonsense.

In no great while, however, as the infirm old King reflected, these silly children would be self-respecting men and women, and this bleating and this pawing at their companions would be put aside for warfare and housework and other sensible matters. Those inter-locked young hands would be parted, the one hand to kill honorably, with fine sword strokes, in a wellbred mêlée of gentlemen, and the other hand to scrub stew-pans and wash diapers. And that would be an excellent outcome: for, to old Alfgar's finding, the unrestrained-ness of these semi-public endearments, through its callow feeble-mindedness, appeared an insult to intelligence.

Then Alfgar saw a woman who walked alone, upon a gravelled walkway, beneath the maples and the syca-more trees of this garden. She came toward the old wanderer, and a jangling and a skirling noise came with her, so that Alfgar knew this was indeed Ettarre. He heard again that music which sought and could not find its desire in any quarter of earth.

But the ears which time had given him got no delight from this music. It seemed, to this decrepit king of men, an adolescent and whining and morbid music. He did not like these noises which seemed to doubt and question everything. It was better to have about you much merrier noises than were these noises, in the while that as yet remained for an aging frail old fellow to be hearing any noises at all.

She was near him now. And Ettarre, he found, was well enough to look at, but in no way remarkable: for to the eyes which time had given him the face of one woman was very much like that of any other woman. Nevertheless, this was his appointed lady in domnei. So the gaunt vagabond knelt, and he kissed the hands of this girl who appeared, after all, quite nice looking, in an unpretentious fashion.

He knelt because this was the Ettarre who had drawn Alfgar out of the set ways of life, and who had stripped him of all that well-thought-of monarchs desired. It was in order that he might kneel here at the feet of his appointed lady in domnei, among the very many small stones which were in this gravelled walkway, that a King of Ecben had put out of men's memory his pre-eminent name.

It was in order to be hurting his thin old knees, with these little rocks' sharp edges, that he had given up his tall throne builded of apple-wood with rivets of copper, and the King of Ecben's four houses builded of white polished stone, with all their noble furnishings, and their fertile gardens and orchards, and their low-lying, red-roofed stables; and he had given up, too, his big golden sceptre with the five kinds of rubies in it, and his herds of fine speckled cattle at Pen Loegyr, and all the pretty shaping and the bright colors of Ettaine, the daughter of Thordis Bent-Neck.

105

These things Alfgar had yielded up not all unwillingly, because of his magnanimous old notions. These
things he had put far behind him, so that he might
be following after that Ettarre whom a poet fetched
from out of the Waste Beyond the Moon, to be alike the
derider and the prey and the destroyer of mankind. Of
all these things the witch-woman had bereft King Alfgar,
and of all other things save only that dream which yet
ruled defiantly in the old wanderer's brave heart.

"Thus then is the quest ended," Alfgar said, after he
had risen up from kneeling upon the edges of those
more and yet more uncomfortable small stones. "I have
kept faith with the old way of Ecben, and with you also
I have kept faith."

The girl answered: "You have kept faith, instead,
with Alfgar, after your own fashion, and after no fashion
which befitted a well-thought-of monarch."

Now Alfgar went on speaking with the quiet pertinacity of an old man; and he spoke, too, as though
he were a little, but not very deeply, puzzled by a
matter of no really grave importance, saying:

"So have I won to you who are my lady in domnei
and my heart's desire. But I am aged now, and it is as
your playfellow said: time has laid hold of me with
both hands, and with the weak remnants of my mortal
body's strength I may neither take nor defend you
as befits a king of men. The music that I once delighted
in seems only a thin vexing now. And my infirm eyes
may not ever again perceive that beauty which my heart
remembers."

The girl replied: "Yet even from the first, my friend,

106

you followed after a music which you could not hear, and after a shining to which your eyes were dimmed. All that which other men desire you have given up because of a notion in which you did not ever quite believe. Yes: you have clung—in your own fashion,—to the old way of Ecben."

He said, "And for that reason, I am content."

She answered him with that cool, and yet condoning, bright gaze which women keep for the strange notions of men. She answered him with words also, saying:

"Yet so have you raised up a brutish and lewd Ulf to the throne of Ecben. So have you tumbled down the god of Ecben. So have you lost that Ettaine for whom your love was human and convenient to the ways of men. So do you stand here, an aged outcast, from whom all ecstasy has departed. So ends the King of Ecben's questing after his vain dream, in folly and wide hurt."

He replied: "Yet am I content. For I have served that dream which I elected to be serving. It may be that no man is royal, and that no god is divine, and that our mothers and our wives have not any part in holiness. Oh, yes, it very well may be that I have lost honor and applause, and that I take destruction, through following after a dream which has in it no truth. Yet my dream was noble; and its nobility contents me."

To that the girl returned, rather sadly, "Alas, my friend, but it is an imagining at which Heaven laughs; and the gray Norns do not fulfil that dream for any man."

Alfgar replied:"Then men are better than that power which made them. For the kings of men do not laugh at this dream: and in the heart of every person that is royal this dream may be fulfilled, even in the while that his body fails and perishes."

"Yet," said Ettarre, "yet, as the strength of a man's mortal body fails, so do his desires perish also. It is a thing more sad than any other thing which men know about, that under the touch of time even they who serve with the most ardor men's highest fancies must lose, a little by a little, all hunger and all faith as to that which is beyond and above them."

He now looked somewhat wistfully into this girl's quite nicely colored and shaped face which was, to him, so like the face of any other young woman who has good health. The gaunt old man flung back his head. His white hair fluttered about in the dawn wind, untidily, and the pale-colored eyes of the tricked wanderer had a vexed and tormented shining, in the while that he said:

"It is not a true thing which you are speaking. For I retain my faith in that which is beyond and above me. I have lost the desire and the vision: but I retain my faith. I retain my faith in that beauty which I may not see, and in that music which I may not hear ever any more, and in that dream which has betrayed me. And I am content."

The girl answered, "You speak without wisdom; for it is not permitted that any man who has heard my music should remain content."

With that, she clasped for one moment his withered hands between her hands, and the witch-woman said very tenderly:

"Most brave and steadfast, and most foolish, of all them who have followed after Ettarre, the gods do well to smile at your strange and fond imaginings. And yet, tall king of men, the gods provide for him that holds to his faith."

She touched his ears. Her finger tips fell lightly upon his wrinkled eyelids.

9. THE CHANGING OF
ALFGAR ❦

ALL things were changed for Alfgar. He was not
any longer a frail and aged person, now that contentment had gone out of him. For all his stoical, enforced
contentment had now made room for joy, because his
youth had returned to him; and in that garden, now,
exulted that Alfgar who had been foremost among the
warriors of Ecben, the Alfgar who had been the most
powerful of kings and the most ardent of lovers and the
most knightly of champions.

All things were changed for Alfgar. He noted, with
imperious young eyes, that lilies abounded to each side
of him, and that in this garden many climbing white
roses also were lighted by the clear and tempered radiancy of early dawn. White rabbits were frisking about
King Alfgar. He saw that the world was lovely, and that
time was friendly to all lovers. He heard a music which
was not of this world, and it sought and could not
find its desire in any quarter of earth. But now was inter-
mingled with this music the sound of doves that called
to their mates; and in this music he found no doubtfulness and no discontent, but only the dear promise of a
life which presently would be created out of the resistless
might of this music's yearning, and which would be
more noble than had been any life yet known to human
kind.

All things were changed for Alfgar, who grasped
with strong hands the hands of the most lovely of the

women who are not quite of this world. For this was visibly that ever-young Ettarre whom very far in the future the magic of a poet's love and the wizardry of mathematics had fetched from out of the Waste Beyond the Moon. to be the delight and the ruin of many human lovers less fortunate than Alfgar had been, and to elude them eternally. But Alfgar she could not elude, he knew, because of those strong hands which held her hands securely.

"The gods provide," said Alfgar, joyously, "for him that holds to his faith!"

So was it that all things were changed for Alfgar through the touch of the witch-woman who had drawn him out of the set ways of life into the garden between dawn and sunrise, and whose magic is more great than is the magic of time. And now from all quarters of the garden whereinto time had not yet entered came young lovers, two by two, in high rejoicing.

They rejoiced because, once more, the gray Norns had regarded respectfully the importance of a sincere love-affair, and because the oncoming years, as is customary, were laboring to reward the steadfastness of true love with never-ending fame and contentment. They cried aloud to Alfgar, with friendly smiles and with gay caperings,—

"The gods provide for him that holds to his faith!"

Then they all praised Alfgar cordially. Each couple said, with the most sympathizing kind of politeness, that Alfgar and his appointed lady in domnei were more remarkable and more glorious than any other pair of lovers who had ever existed, saving only one pair—

which pair no couple was so egotistic as to mention out-right.

They that had served Ettarre came also, all those maimed poets whose living she had ruined. And they said:

"Hail and farewell, Ettarre! Because of you, we could be contented with no woman. We turned away from that frank and wholesome world wherein frank, wholesome maidens walked amiably along sunlit ways. We perceived that the younger females of our kind were pleasant to the touch and were agreeably tinted. But we turned away, we blundered into more murky places, and we got deep scarrings there, because these maids were not as was that witch-woman whom we had seen and might not forget. As moths flitter after torches, so did we pursue your lost loveliness, to our own hurt."

And these poets said also:

"Because of your music, we could get no delight from the music of our verses nor from any melody that is of this world. We were enamored of a music which no words might entrap or cage. There was a music which had no fault in it, as we well knew, because we had heard such music once, for a little while. But no man who lived upon earth might recapture that music. The cradle-songs of the fond mothers who bore us were less dear than was that music. The pipes and the organs and the fiddles made no such music. We heard the trumpets and the harps and the clarions; we heard the church bells; and we were not comforted."

Then these poets said:

"Because of you, we lived among mankind as exiles.

The emperors and the captains perceived that we did not regard their famousness as a weighty matter. The priests and the well-thought-of sages perceived that in the while they instructed us our minds were upon a mystery, and that our thinking cherished a legend which was not their legend. So the strong derided us, and said lightly that we were wit-stricken: but, in their troubled hearts, they hated us. For we went among them as men who had drunk wine from a goblet of fairy gold: the wholesome fare of earth may not content such men: and to all human kind they become abhorrent."

Whereafter these maimed poets cried out very fondly:

"Yet we who never found contentment in any hour of our living, all we who followed after you to our own hurt, we would have nothing changed. That loveliness which we saw once and then lost forever, and that music which we heard and shall not ever hear again, were things more fine than is contentment. Hail and farewell, Ettarre!"

Such was the speaking of these poets, and so was it that they all made ready for the marriage feast of Alfgar the high king and Ettarre the most fair of those women who are not quite of this world.

10. THE WAY IT ENDED

*I*T WAS now that Horvendile came likewise. As he had done in Alfgar's dream, so now did this red-headed young man smile without any mirth; and he laid the hand of Ettarre in the hand of Alfgar, in the while that the lean youngster was speaking a word of power.

Then Alfgar grasped exultingly, with his strong arms, the wife that he had won, and his lips touched her lips. It was in this instant the young face of Horvendile became white and drawn. It is not well to give where one desires.

And in the same instant the maimed servitors of Ettarre had vanished, and all the beautiful and merry young lovers passed in a many-colored mistiness. But to these had succeeded a wonder-working yet more amiable, for in this garden three immortals now sat watching Alfgar with complacence.

The largest of these smiling gods was broad-browed and great-eyed, with very long black hair and a thick beard: the robe which he wore was fashioned out of five hundred and forty and three goatskins; and with his left hand he carried a spear of flickering fire. The second god was clothed in red, striped with fine flickering lines of white; and in his yellow hair were two white plumes; between the thumb and the forefinger of his left hand he held a white bull, as yet only partially eaten. But the third god was copper-colored. He was by so much the least of the divine three that, now they all sat cross-legged upon the ground, his head rose but a little way above the taller locust-trees of the garden. About his

114

head flew swallows. He was naked save that wrapped everywhere around his body was a darkly gleaming snake which whispered into the ear of its master with an ever flickering tongue.

Such were the appearances of Kuri and of Uwardowa and of Kogi, who were the supreme gods of Rorn. Each of them was smiling now that Alfgar had won his heart's desire. It was a great joy to Alfgar to see that these Divine Ones bore toward him no grudge, but that instead each god had lifted up his right hand, in blessing and forgiveness.

Then these gods arose and went away laughing. The power was not yet gone out of them.

It was in this way that the garden between dawn and sunrise was emptied of all living creatures save Ettarre and Horvendile; and that at their feet you saw, still faintly simmering, that which the pleasure of the gods of Rorn had left of King Alfgar.

AN EPILOGUE AS TO OTHER WANDERERS ₰

*T*HE gods provide for him that holds to his faith,"
said Horvendile, with a slow smiling. "These jealous
and these rather pig-headed Heavenly Ones have very
smoothly rounded off our playing with this tall, over-
faithful fool: and so the saga of King Alfgar, after all,
ends neatly enough."

But Ettarre did not smile. "This man was better
and more fine than we are. I would that I could weep
for this brave outcast king of men whose folly was
more noble than is our long playing. Dear Horvendile,
and why may you give me no human heart?"

The eternal artist looked sadly toward her who was
the pulse of all his dreams' desire, in the while that she
waited there beyond the blackened and ruined body
of King Alfgar. "And why may you give me no happiness, Ettarre, such as—in this tall fool's one moment,—
you gave to him?"

Thereafter Horvendile parted from the witch-woman,
but not for long. For all happiness must end with death,
and all that which is human must die. But Horvendile
and his Ettarre, they who are neither happy nor quite
human, may not, so does their legend tell us, ever die;
nor as yet have they parted from each other for the last
time.

And as yet, so does this legend recite furthermore,
it remains their doom that he only of her lovers may

not hope to win Ettarre, even though it is permitted he should not wholly lose her, as must mortal men who approach thus near to the witch-woman lose her eternally, along with all else which they possess.

Some say this Horvendile is that Madoc who first fetched Ettarre from out of the gray Waste Beyond the Moon, to live upon our earth in many handsomely colored bodies. The truth of this report is not certainly known. But it is known that these two pass down the years in a not ever ending severance which is their union. It is known that in their passing they allure men out of the set ways of life, and so play with the lives of men for their diversion. As they beguiled Alfgar, so have these beguiled a great sad host of other persons, upon whom Horvendile and Ettarre have put a summoning for their diversion's sake, lest these two immortals should think too heavily about their own doom.

To those men from whom they get their sport they give a moment of contentment. But Horvendile and his Ettarre have only an unfed desire as they pass down the years together; and because of that knowledge which they share, hope does not travel with them, nor do they get from their playing any joy. For each of these tricked lovers knows that each is but an empty shining, and that, thus, each follows after the derisive shadow of a love which the long years have not made real.

EXPLICIT

117

THE
WHITE ROBE

A SAINT'S SUMMARY

*"Righteousness shall be the girdle of his loins,
and faithfulness the girdle of his reins;
and the wolf shall dwell with the lamb."*

FOR

FRANCES NEWMAN

—inevitably—this story of dead lovers that were faithful

1. OF HIS MANNER OF LIFE
IN THE SECULAR STATE &

*H*EREWITH begins the history of that Odo, called Le Noir, who nevertheless, even as the morning star makes light the womb of a black cloud, shone with the bright beams of his life and teaching; who by his radiance led into the light them that shivered in the gray cloud of the shadow of death; and who, like unto the rainbow giving light in the white clouds, set forth in his righteous ending the seal of his fond Master's covenant.

His life, or legend, narrates at outset that Odo had tended the sheep of Guillaume Diaz for nearly a year before he went into the Druid wood which is called Bovion, with Pierre la Charonne. It was thus that, under an elm tree, young Odo, who was as yet a little stained with the dust of his worldly journeying, first saw the Lord of the Forest.

That dark Master gave a wolf skin to each of the boys and a pot of ointment with which a man might anoint his body whensoever he was wearied of inhabiting it. The Master, also, after they had made a covenant with him and had tendered homage to both of his faces, baptized the boys, after the quaint formula of his very old religion, with the new and secret names of Prettyman and Princox.

After that, the pair used to run coursing in the shape of wolves until, in the unfortunate manner tiffs come about so quickly out of the hot-headed play of youth,

123

the two lads quarreled one night over a particularly fine heifer. They fought; and after Odo had feasted upon two delicacies instead of one, then Black Odo hunted alone.

The best time for this joyous gaming, he found, was an hour or a half-hour before dawn when the moon was on the wane. The lustiness of his chosen overlord was then at prime; and those relatively parvenu gods and archangels, as yet precariously perched up in heaven, seemed not strong enough to deal with rebels. It was then that Odo used to snarl and yelp his praise of the kindly power which enabled him without any hindrance to enjoy the most profound and soul-stirring delights. He exulted, as a zealous Old Believer, thus to attest the strength and shrewdness of his dark Master, which could outwit so cunningly their celestial adversaries.

At this season Odo le Noir went as an animal somewhat shorter and stouter than a real wolf, with a smaller head, a pronged tail, and a rather reddish pelt. He diverted himself with sheep and dogs and cattle of all kinds, but the young of his own race he found to be the daintiest hunting.

There was no little gossip, and some serious complaint, about the wild beast which was ravaging the Val-Ardray district, because, with the habitual impetuosity of youth, Black Odo kept no measure in his recreations. The ill-nourished cattle and children of the lower classes were of no large value. But, at Nointel, Odo had entered the Lord of Basardra's home, and, finding no one there except the Countess' last baby, in its gilded and blue-veiled cradle, he had seized and carried off this really important sprig of nobility; and by-and-by, behind a hedge in the garden, he left the remainder of the ruined small body to be discovered, as it happened, by the Lord of Basardra himself. No nobleman could view without displeasure the untidiness of such freedoms with his offspring.

Odo created even more scandal, however, when near Lisuarte he attacked the Castellan's daughter, a charming and delightfully plump young lady of eleven. Her also he put out of living, by-and-by. But everyone knew there had been something irregular about the affair, because her white and red garments were not torn in quite the way that they would have been if wolves born of a wolf's body had made the assault; and only the lower portions of her belly had been eaten.

Thus for a while Odo le Noir lived very merrily and was obedient to no one save the Lord of the Forest. This loving master initiated the boy into old and elaborate diversions, and he promised an even finer future.

"I design great things for you, my Prettyman," the Master would assure Black Odo, "and I intend that you shall go far in the service to which we are both enlisted."

2. OF HIS ARDENT LOVE AND APPROACH TO MARTYRDOM ૐ

*N*ow in these years Ettarre was living, in the appearance of a peasant girl, at the foot of the hills behind Perdigon, and she made her home in the thatched hut of an ancient couple who regarded and treated her as their own child. They loved their fosterling; they did not suspect that she had been fetched from the gray spaces behind the moon to live upon earth, in many bodies, as the eternal victim and the eternal derider of all human poets who for a stinted season have youth in their hearts; and, in fact, there was at this time no talk of any sort about Ettarre, except that here and there people said she was one of the witches of Amneran.

At this time also, on an April afternoon, in open daylight, a wolf attacked the peasant girl Ettarre while she was watching the cow and the four sheep. She defended herself boldly with the fallen branch of an oak tree. After that, the stout reddish-colored animal drew back and sat down like a dog upon his haunches, at a more comfortably remote distance, of about twelve paces, and thence looked at her for a moment or two. A thrush chirped and twittered overhead. The wolf presently yawned; he trotted away; and Ettarre at supper mentioned, as a curious circumstance, that the beast's tail was pronged.

It was just after this that young Odo le Noir began

his courtship of Ettarre the peasant girl, whom some believed to be a witch-woman, and now the boy followed her everywhither.

"Most charming Ettarre! my own heart's darling!" he would say, "there was never anybody who was more white and tender than is your body."

"But you, Black Odo, are much too dark for my taste."

"I did not speak of taste, Ettarre. Yet your bright eyes so dazzle me that I know not of what I am speaking."

"Your eyes, Black Odo, are too strange and deep-set. When, as so rarely happens, you look straight into my face, then your wild eyes, Black Odo, are made horrible by that red and flaring light which shows behind them."

"Do you not laugh at me, Ettarre, but let us two be friends after the manner of the friendly beasts!"

"I would not have you laugh, black beast; for your teeth are long and sharp, and I loathe the sight of them."

"Yet is my hunger for you very great—"

"And what is that to me, whose dislike of you is so much greater?"

"Let us touch hands, then, in farewell!"

"Not even your hand will I touch willingly, Black Odo, for your finger-nails are unpleasantly long and like the claws of a wolf."

With that, the beautiful young girl fled away from him, across a meadow where cowslips grew. It seemed to Odo that a strange and troubling music followed after her. In any case, this meeting was but a sample of many other meetings. And never at any time would Ettarre listen to his wooing; but the boy Odo continued to desire this peasant girl.

Yet his most deep desires were for the Lord of the Forest, and for the delights which they shared in the Druid wood, and for the even larger gustos that were to be the rewards of Odo's fearlessness by-and-by.

"I design great things for you, my Prettyman," the Master would assure him, "and I intend that you shall go far in the service to which we are both enlisted."

Even after Odo had been seized, and in the while that he lay in the dark prison at Lisuarte, the Master would come to him at night, and would fondle him, and would repeat this assurance.

3. OF HIS CONFESSION AND CONVERSION ❧

BLACK ODO was brought before the criminal court at Yair. He confessed everything, and departed from the truth only in saying it was Ettarre the wicked witchwoman, who had seduced his innocence; who had first led him to the Lord of the Forest; and who upon three occasions had rubbed him all over with the ointment and helped him into the wolf skin. But Ettarre, after she also had been fetched to Yair, would confess nothing. Her stubbornness was a calamity to the patience of her judges: yet these earnest men did not despair, but they tortured her white flesh again and again, even until she died, in their long-suffering attempts to win the obstinate girl to candor and repentance.

The tweezers and hammers and hot irons were not needed in cross-examining Odo, because he confessed freely whatsoever any one of his black-robed judges suggested, and then went edifyingly far beyond any merely judicial imaginings. Odo, called Le Noir, was therefore found guilty upon all counts.

Messire Gui de Puysange, president of the court, pronounced the sentence. His long fingers played idly with the large silver inkstand before him in the while that he was speaking. He pointed out that, thanks to the progress of science, in the enlightened age whose benefits they were all sharing, lycanthropy, or that form of mania in which the patient imagined himself to be, and acted as, a wolf, was now known to be an hallucination, or, as some learned persons thought, a form of chronic insanity; and, in either case, was, to the eyes of the considerate, more properly an affliction than a crime. The said Odo, called Le Noir, in consequence, and in consideration of his youth and of the corrupting influence exerted by his deceased paramour, and in consideration of his lack of educational advantages, should be sent to the monastery at Aigremont, for better restraint and rearing, and for the re-establishment of his mental and spiritual health, said Messire de Puysange. Science, gentlemen, said Messire de Puysange, science was at last, in these progressive times, teaching us how to deal sanely with the insane.

Over this rather neat epigram, felt generally to be a credit to the bench, his confrères blinked and nodded like a roosting line of benevolent owls. But the condemned boy wept a little. Youth parts from its illusions with pain; and Odo saw that it was his dear Lord of the Forest who, in a long black gown and a curled mountain of blond hair, was pronouncing this sentence, so that Odo knew the Master was only the head of the coven of Amneran, a mere sorcerer, and not the glorious being whom Odo had thought him.

So it was that the blessed Odo, as yet a little stained with the dust of his worldly journeying, lost faith in evil as a dependable ally.

Now for what seemed to him a long while Black Odo was not happy in the Monastery of St. Hoprig, but went about on all fours, eating only such food as he could find upon the ground. He still craved the delights of his nocturnal hunting; he thought especially about small girls;

130

and constantly he was hoping it would not be long before he had another taste of the food he desired. Yet
by-and-by, a little by a little, he grew reconciled to the
quiet and easy life of the monastery.

He became interested in religious matters. He delighted in particular to have the good monks tell him
about the suffering of the saints upon this wicked earth,
and how these holy persons had been broiled and flayed
and hacked into quivering mince-meat for their faith's
sake. When he listened to these stories he sat huddled,
with his legs crossed very tightly. At times his shoulders
twitched convulsively. Then the boy would growl, and
he would wipe away the white foam which was drib-
bling thinly from the corners of his mouth.

Young Odo, too, was never wearied of discussing with
his religious instructors the cunning torments which the
damned must suffer eternally: and of the more intimate
details of these tortures he began to speak with a fervor
which was truly devout. In fine, grace entered into his
heart; he desired to become an officially accredited
servant of Heaven; and the order of St. Hoprig gladly
received this most notable brand from the burning.

Sometimes, even after the novice had entered into his
holy vocation, the Lord of the Forest would come to him
in the night time, saying as of old,—

"I design great things for you, my Prettyman."

But Brother Odo could not forget how basely this Gui
de Puysange had deceived him, and how the dark and
withered sorcerer had abused the faith of an innocent
boy, by pretending to be the all-powerful Master of Evil.
So Odo would make the sign of the cross, he would re-

peat the sacred Latin words, and he would thus force his tempter to depart.

And old Gui de Puysange would say: "You treat me very cruelly, my Prettyman. Nevertheless, I love you, and because of that covenant which is between us my love shall yet cherish you vicariously."

4. OF THE DIVINE CONDESCEN-
SIONS SHOWN UNTO HIM ॐ

BROTHER ODO increased in sanctity. He was blessed
with religious fervors, such as the Devil so cunningly
mimics with epilepsy, in which the inspired young
devotee's disregard of the flesh caused him to bite and
claw at the bodies of all those who came to assist him
from the pavement or the walkway where he was writh-
ing in pious ecstasy. He was granted also the biliousness
and the upset digestion needful to create an all-over-
bearing ardor against any compromise with the soft and
wheedling ways of evil. A slight hiccough continually
interrupted his talking, as his stomach was relieved of
gas. He was accorded visions in which he was counselled
and instructed by many saints.

These came to confirm the holy man in his faith by
showing him from what sins and perversities they themselves had been rescued by faith who now were saints
in the higher courts of Paradise.

"Such were the customs of my wicked way of living
in Augsburg," said St. Eutropia, "before the grace of
Heaven visited me."

"It was in this way I paid the ferryman with my
body's beauty," said St. Mary the Egyptian, "in order
that I might get to Jerusalem and obtain salvation."

"Such was the form of loathsome and unnatural caress
for which I was particularly notorious," said St. Margaret of Cortona, "before I found repentance and true
faith."

133

All these sacred events the blessed saints would rehearse, with Brother Odo's aid, so that he might perceive with his own senses from how poisonously sweet and how affable iniquities the most vile of sinners might yet be rescued, and brought into eternal glory, by the true faith.

Even better was to follow, in Heaven's tender furtherance of the welfare of Heaven's loving and vigorous servant. For in a while Ettarre, the reputed witch-woman whom Brother Odo had once so ardently desired, and whom communion with no saint had ever quite put out of his mind, now also came to him.

And it was a queer thing, too, that with the coming of Ettarre the appearance of his cell was changed into the appearance of a quiet-colored garden. Lilies seemed to abound everywhere in this garden, and many climbing white roses, also, which were lighted by a clear and tempered radiancy like that of dawn. Moreover, a number of white rabbits were frisking about Brother Odo, and he could hear the sound of doves that called to their mates very softly.

With such a pleasant miracle did Ettarre return to Brother Odo from out of that celestial estate which he had procured for this beautiful girl by contriving her martyrdom. She came to assure him of her gratitude in all possible ways. After that, nobody was happier, night after night, than was Brother Odo.

And in the day time he preached everywhere what these noble ladies had descended from Paradise to teach him. He in particular denounced the impertinences of science,—"of science so called," as Brother Odo impressively and scathingly described the snare which evil sets for human self-conceit,—and he taught that through faith and divine election lay the one way to salvation. He became the glory of the monastery. The white-robed Abbot declared that of all his children in the spirit Odo was the most worthy to be his successor.

5. OF HIS YET FURTHER
INCREASE IN GRACE ❧

*N*OR, when Odo had been anointed as Abbot of St. Hoprig, and went clothed in the white woolen robe of his office, did he cease from reproving evil-doers with unflinching severity. Yet so merciful was the new Abbot that no offender was permitted to die in a state of sin whensoever that could be avoided. Instead, the Abbot would prolong painstakingly the more concrete arguments of the Church so as to win for every backslider and every heretic sufficient time in which to repent and thus to be spared from suffering in the next world.

The Abbot himself would carry humbly his own easy-chair into the torture chamber, and would watch over the torments, lest death end them too speedily, even by one instant, for his erring brother's real and eternal good. Very often his dinner was brought to him in the torture chamber, and he would eat it there, among the most unappetizing sights and screams and odors, rather than neglect, even for an instant, his spiritual duties.

Nor could you have found anywhere a more eloquent preacher. The Abbot's sermons made converts right and left, because he so frightened his hearers that no one of them dared risk that Hell of which this blessed gaunt man told them very lovingly. He spoke of Hell's perpetual and unquenchable fires, of Hell's pitch and brimstone and toads and adders, of Hell's horrible hot mists and of giant gray worms which fed upon the broiled damned, and he imitated quite effectively the hoarse howling of lost souls when devils toss them about on muck forks. He spoke of all these things with the particularity of one who rejoiced in these strong discouragements of laxity in well-doing. He appalled his auditors with that faithful rendering of every unpleasant detail which is the essence of realism.

So great was the Abbot's ardor that in his eyes awoke a red flaring, and a white foam would dribble thinly from his lips, in the while that he called sinners to repentance and spoke of the blood of the Lamb. He thus frightened many of the more impressionable into convulsions; some died of terror; but the survivors crept tremblingly into the sustaining arms of Holy Church, which alone could save them from these torments.

Meanwhile the Abbot labored, too, to convict old Gui de Puysange of his abominable practices. The Abbot labored the more zealously because of that dim yearning and that terrible tenderness which moved in the heart of the white-robed Abbot whensoever he beheld this dark and withered sorcerer. He labored, though, because of this vile wizard's circumspection, without any success; and blessed Odo could secure no proof that this reprobate was one of the Old Believers, until through Heaven's grace the well-nigh despairing Abbot was accorded a revelation in this matter.

"Good may very well come of that which merely mortal reason finds blameworthy," Ettarre declared one night, after the Abbot of St. Hoprig had reached a state of comparative dejection, "for the divinely elect serve Heaven's will and the true welfare of their fellow beings with every manner of tool. Do you, my darling, who are one of these peculiarly favored persons, but think, for example, of how with perjury you brought about my ascension into the delights of Paradise! By an action which many of the unsanctified might esteem contemptible you then purchased for me such joys, my dearest Odo, that I sometimes leave them half-unwillingly even to come to you."

The Abbot beat and tore at her white tender flesh, but only with his hands, until she confessed that nowhere in Paradise had she found any joys more dear to her than those they were sharing. Nevertheless, upon reflection, he fairmindedly admitted the logic of his celestial bedfellow's argument.

Therefore, an hour or two before dawn, he coursed abroad, toward the home of old Gui de Puysange, at Ranec, in the appearance of a stout and reddish-colored animal. There was a quite serviceable moon. The blessed Odo met, at first, no living creature save a real wolf, a virgin female, who accepted him as one of her own kind. Presently they coursed together: and the grateful Abbot snarled and yelped his praise of the kindly Heaven which enabled him, over and yet over again, but without any sinfulness, to enjoy the most profound and soul-stirring delights. He exulted, as a zealous Churchman, thus to attest the strength and shrewdness of Heaven, which could outwit so cunningly their infernal adversaries.

6. OF HIS CONTINUED ZEAL AND EFFICACY &

*T*HE next day a mangled baby was found in the back garden of Messire de Puysange, and the evidence against him was so made legally complete. Old Gui de Puysange was tried that month, with the white-robed Abbot of St. Hoprig sitting as president of the court; and the accused man was duly condemned to be burned as a werewolf.

Messire de Puysange did not complain. He knew that this was the appointed ninth year for the sacrifice, and that he himself had incited this inevitable sacrifice through the illusions which he had sent to amuse the sleeping of Odo.

"I had vaingloriously designed great things for you, my Prettyman," this dark and withered sorcerer said at the last, in the market-place, when they were heaping up the faggots about him. "But my arts end with me. There will be no more saints to counsel and to cherish you, as my vicars. Never any more, so long as you wear mortal flesh, will there be any pretty Sendings, my Prettyman, now that the Prince of this world receives his sacrifice."

The Abbot was troubled; for he now knew that all the consolations of his piety had been the vicars of this persistent sorcerer. The Abbot's hand went to his chin, and he hiccoughed slightly, but he did not say anything.

Then dark old Gui de Puysange, looking up toward the Abbot Odo, with patient and adoring brown eyes, said fondly:

"Yet there will be one more Sending to convey you home. Meanwhile you, my dear, in your white robe—which once was but the clothing of a witless sheep,—have not any need of my aid, to go further than I might fare in the service to which we are both enlisted."

And again, a terrible, a treacherous and a damnable sort of yearning and tenderness was troubling the white-robed Abbot, as he looked, now for the last time, upon the fettered wretch who once had so ignobly deceived an innocent boy by pretending to be the all-powerful Master of Evil, and who now had deceived a well-thought-of clergyman with illusive Sendings in the appearance of saints. But decorum has to be preserved in the pursuit of every profession.

So the enthroned and white-robed Abbot, it is recorded, only frowned a little at this unseemly interruption of the impressive ceremony which so many of the faithful had assembled to witness. After that, he gave the signal to the torch-bearers. He settled back in his tall cushioned chair of carved teak-wood and Yemen leather, under the blue and yellow canopy which this unpleasantly warm day necessitated; and he watched pensively the ending of the one person whom he had loved with an entire heart.

7. OF THE SALUTARY POWER
OF HIS PREACHING ⁊

*T*HEREAFTER the Abbot found that Messire de Puysange had indeed spoken the truth. Abbot Odo was denied the consolations of religion. No more visions came
to him from out of Paradise. He was counselled and
instructed by no more saints.

He understood that all these had been vicarious illusions provided by the loving arts of dark and withered
Gui de Puysange. The Abbot comprehended that he was
not immortal; that there was no Heaven and no Hell;
that there would be no auditing of human accounts; and
that he travelled, instead, toward annihilation. His biliousness left him, his digestion became perfect, now
that he perceived men perish as the beasts perish, and
now that he knew every form of religion was a cordial
which sustained people through the tedium and discomfort of their stay upon earth.

For he could well perceive the value of human faith
now that he had lost it. He spoke everywhere of God's
love for all men and of how gloriously Heaven was to
be won through repentance and a putting away of disreputable habits. He inflicted few tortures nowadays,
because in Abbot Odo had awakened the fervor of the
elect artist who respects the medium of his craft.
. . . Dear Gui had been an artist of sorts, the Abbot
would reflect, in the great-hearted poor fellow's limited
field, with his peculiarly small audience of one. Yes, Gui
de Puysange had created wholly creditable saints, who

141

were finished to the last detail. . . . But the art of a self-respecting clergyman was more general and more noble in its scope, for it appealed to the dull-witted and the unhappy everywhere.

With gaping hundreds to attend him, Abbot Odo swayed the minds of his congregation at will, and he awakened joy and faith, not with the tricks of black magic, not any longer with heated irons and tweezers, but with very lovely words. Since he knew there was no Hell, he hardly ever threatened people with Hell's pains: instead, he turned from realism to romance, and he improvised brilliantly as to the unfathomable love and the eternal bliss of Heaven, which was the heritage of mankind and awaited every communicant just beyond the tomb. His talking aroused his auditors to the best and purest emotions.

His fame spread. He was summoned to court. The King was greatly moved by the Abbot's fine sermons, and swore by the belly of St. Gris that this holy man had fire in his belly. The ladies of the court did not approve of this metaphor, but they all found the Abbot of St. Hoprig adorable.

"Especially," said one of them, "when one's husband, alas—!"

"But, darling," cried her friend, "do you mean that you also—?"

"I mean only that if only other men—"

"Yet only a clergyman, my pet, can give you absolution—"

"—Like a digestant tablet—"

"Ah, but one dines so heartily with the dear Abbot—"

Thus did these ladies chatter under their little ermine
bonnets and their three-cornered lattice caps and their
glittering cauls of silver net wire. So the Abbot of St.
Hoprig was a vast social success; he had the entrée everywhere; and he made converts right and left.

The Queen herself confessed to him: and after he had
gone thoroughly into the personal affairs of this daughter of the Medici and had lovingly absolved her, she
saw to it forthwith that this wonderful man was appointed Bishop of Valnères.

8. OF THE KINDLY IMPULSES
OF HIS PIETY ☙

*I*N THE episcopal palace the blessed Odo lived at his
ease very happily. He did not miss the company of his
saints now that so many of the parish needed to be con-
soled and comforted by a bishop who, after all, was
aging; and the loss of his own faith was a great aid to
him now that it was his métier to awaken faith in so
many others. It was a loss which made for unfailing tact
without dogmatism. It was a loss which had ridded him
forever of those doubts which sometimes trouble the
clergy.

For Odo of Valnères lived as an artist. His contentment was here, rather than in any perhaps unattainable
places or in any contingently oncoming times. And he
made sure of it by creating contentment in every person
about him.

Throughout all Naimousin and Piémontais he cherished his little flock as the father cherishes his children,
and the artist his audience. He saw to their bodily com-
forts, he saw above all to their faith. For the plight of
the lower orders of mankind, he knew, demanded just
this faith which was, for a being of a peasant's or a shop-
keeper's far from admirable nature, at once a narcotic
and a beneficial restraint.

An altruist would dissuade therefore the evilly in-
clined from all incivic vices like murder and rape and
theft and arson which, even when practised upon an
international scale and under the direct patronage of the

144

Church, tended always to upset the comfort of society. An altruist would endeavor, to the untrammeled extent of his imaginative gifts, to sustain the cowardly and the feeble-minded, and the aged and the ill and the poverty-stricken, and all other persons who were unbearably afflicted by the normal workings of the laws of life and of human polity. An altruist would hearten all these luckless beings with the appropriate kind of romances about an oncoming heritage which made the dear poor wretches' present transitory discomforts—from any really considerate point of view—quite unimportant.

It was therefore, to the now aging Bishop, whensoever he put on his mitre and the white linen robe of his office, a privilege and a delight to preach of faith and hope and charity to his little flock. These frightened, foolish, and yet rather lovable men and women did need so dreadfully, in their cheerless and thwarted living, the ever-present threat and the ever-present promise of true religious faith to keep them sane or, for that matter, to keep them at all endurable associates. So the Bishop served his art lovingly; he delighted in the exercise of his art: for he saw that religious faith was highly necessary to the well-being of the lower classes, and was serviceable and comforting to the gentry also as one got on in life.

He had few regrets. He regretted Ettarre, the lost witch-woman, because no Christian whom he had ever known, howsoever charitable and zealous, had approached the charm of that little darling when she was pretending to be a saint come out of Paradise. He regretted that it no longer amused him to run abroad in

145

his wolf's skin. Once in a while, of course, that was necessary as a professional duty—after loving kindness and
the customary dole of soup and blankets had failed,—in
order to dispose of some open case of irreligion and ill-
living which afforded a really dangerous example to the
diocese: but such sinners were, almost always, so anæmic
and stringy that the Bishop had come honestly to dislike
this branch of his church-work. In fine, he conceded,
willingly enough, that Odo of Valnères was approach-
ing the end of his middle age; and that his main delights
must be henceforward in his art.

And sometimes he regretted, too, that his art could
not extend to yet other mythologies. He admired the
clearer character drawing of the gods whom he found
in these other mythologies. There were fine themes for
a creative artist in the exalted doings of Zeus, the Cloud-
collecting, the Thunder-hurler, who was called also
Muscarius, because he drove away flies: and in the zo-
ölogical amours of Zeus you would have had an oppor-
tunity for much rich, bold, romantic coloring, with the
flesh tints handsomely rendered.

Then the heroic conception of Ragnarök, that final
and most great of all battles between good and evil—
wherein the Norse gods, and the entire Scandinavian
church militant along with them, were to perish intrep-
idly for the right's sake,—was a theme which, in view
of its sublime possibilities in the pulpit of a sincere artist,
thrilled the reflective Bishop like a trumpet music.

It was a dangerous notion, though, thus to portray
religion as in the end an unprofitable business enter-
prise, which broke up in cosmic bankruptcy; and of

146

course his little flock would never in this world appreciate the tragic heroism of Ragnarök. No: for you had to hearten the middle classes with the prospects of exceedingly shiny rewards which would be eternal, in a golden city that you entered through a gate of pearl. Still, as a theme, the Bishop greatly fancied Ragnarök.

Then, too, the Bishop meditated, how charming it would be, once in a way,—or throughout, perhaps, the entire, rather depressing Lenten season,—to make use of the delightfully quaint effects of African or of Polynesian mythology from his pulpit. One had so rarely, from that restrained and over-sedate eminence, the chance to exercise one's gifts of quiet humor and of that naïveté in which supreme artists alone excel. Yes: it would be wholly pleasant to tell one's little flock about Gajjimarê the Snake God, and about the misadventures of Barin Mūtum after this half-being had borrowed a body for nuptial purposes, and about the wonders which Maui-shaped-in-the-topknot-of-Taranga performed with his great-grandmother's jawbone.

But, after all, the artist must work in that material which is available. After all, Christianity displayed many excellent points and gratifying improvements added since the decease of its founder. And as a theme —whensoever that theme was handled with competence, and touched with true inspiration,—Christianity served handsomely enough to keep one's little flock contented, by assuring them of oncoming rewards for prudent and respectable conduct. No altruist could ask for more.

The Bishop smiled, and got back to his Christmas sermon.

147

THE WITCH-WOMAN

In brief, there was never a more respected nor a more generally beloved bishop in those parts. And it was a great loss to Naimousin and all Piémontais when one morning the blessed Odo quitted the episcopal palace, he did not remember just when or through what agency.

9. OF THE REWARD APPOINTED FOR HIM ॐ

*I*N FACT, it was with something of a shock that the blessed Odo awakened to his unclerical circumstances. To be abroad in his nightgown was bad enough: but it seemed out of reason that, in such informal attire, he should be floating thus through a gray void, upborne by what appeared an unusually thick and soft and gaudily colored rug, and sharing its tenancy with this young woman.

"Can you by any chance inform me, madame," he inquired, with the courtesy for which he was justly famed, "what is the meaning of this exercise in the humorous? and who has had the impudence to put me up here?"

"Do you not fret, poor Odo," she replied. "It is only that you also, my dear, are dead at last."

And then the Bishop recognized her. Then he knew that, somehow, some praiseworthy wonder-working had conveyed him back again to Ettarre, the reputed witch-woman. And for that instant nothing else whatever appeared to matter. For this adorable child seemed lovelier and even more desirable than ever: she was near to him: and age and all the sedative impairments of age had very marvelously gone away from the good Bishop of Val-nères.

Yet in another instant his handsome countenance was a bit vexed; and he looked not altogether happy as he sat

149

upright upon the smallish gold- and salmon-colored cloud.

"Nevertheless," the Bishop said, "nevertheless, this is an illogical situation. I do recall now that I was suffering, very slightly, with indigestion last night. A complete atheist never agrees with me. And at my age, of course— Yes, yes, for me to have passed away in my sleep is natural enough. Yet this continued survival of my consciousness—howsoever surprising and pleasant be the result of that consciousness," he added, with a gallant inclination of his head toward the winsome love of his youth,—"is a very sad blow to science. It upsets all philosophy; and it is a trouble to my common-sense."

"My dearest," replied Ettarre, "you have done with such frivolities as common-sense and philosophy and science; and but for my intervention there would have remained for you, as I must tell you frankly, only some heavenly reward or another."

"Most charming Ettarre! my own heart's darling!" said the Bishop, "let us not jest about professional matters, not just at present, for everything seems quite topsy-turvy here, and I am in no mood for sprightly sallies. So do you instead tell we whither this cloud is conveying us!"

The girl regarded him with a humorous and, yet, a very tender sort of mockery. "Whither, you ask—with that nicety of diction which for so long has characterized your public speaking,—is this cloud conveying us? Well, one must distinguish. I only came for the ride. But you, my dear doomed Odo, are at this moment on your way to the Heaven which you used to promise to your parishioners; and, in fact, you may already see, just yonder, the amethyst ramparts of the Holy City."

"This is surprising beyond words!" said Odo of Valnères. "Dear me, but this is terrible!"

"You will be finding very few to agree with you yonder," Ettarre replied, "where you will find, instead, all that quaint Heaven of yours aflutter in honor of your arrival. For in the eloquent excesses of the fine career just ended you have converted many persons. Indeed, you have allured into eternal salvation—as the Archangel Oriphiel has announced officially in this morning's report,—no less than one thousand and a hundred and seven souls. In consequence, the blessed everywhere are preparing at this instant to welcome home the strong champion of Heaven, with sackbut and with psaltery and with the full resources of the celestial choir."

"Alas!" said blessed Odo, for the second time, "but this is truly terrible!"

And with that, he thoughtfully re-arranged his nightgown, he pulled up more neatly about his ankles his red flannel footwarmers, and he fell into a moment's bewildered pondering. Nobody of his well-known modesty would have believed the total to run to four figures, but his eloquence and his lively flow of imagery had, of course, at odd times, converted many persons into accepting the comforting assurances of religion. Nor could the Bishop detect anything blameworthy in his conduct, even now.

He had acted logically. The plight of the lower orders of mankind, in the world which Odo of Valnères had now left behind him, did very certainly appear to demand this faith which was, for a being of a peasant's or a shop-keeper's far from admirable nature, at once a narcotic and a beneficial restraint.

"In brief, the situation is perplexing," the Bishop said, aloud, "and it presents features which no clergyman could have anticipated. Yet I stay convinced that, if only I had been lying, there would have been no flaw in my conduct."

Now the charming girl, who had cuddled happily beside him, as though once more to be in touch with her dear Odo were all-sufficient to her faithful heart, said nothing, as yet.

But to a well-thought-of bishop, discarnate and adrift in space, clad only in his nightgown and his red flannel footwarmers, it appeared a bit upsetting, thus to find religious notions exceeding their justifiable arena, and pursuing him beyond the grave.

And upon reflection, the unreasonableness of this outcome for his long and honorable career was not its only troubling feature. For Odo of Valnères looked now toward the nearing huge white wharf beyond which gleamed the portal of Heaven. That entrance really was an enormous pearl, with a hole in it for you to go through, and above that hole, as he could now perceive, was carved the name "Levi."

Odo of Valnères recalled his Scriptural studies; and, with augmenting uneasiness, he poked at the plump velvet-soft ribs of his companion upon the little gold-and salmon-colored cloud.

"Do you wake up, my darling Ettarre, and tell me if this place is much like the Biblical description!"

The lovely girl sat up obediently.

"The Kingdom of Heaven is as Jehovah created it, and as His Scriptures have revealed it," said Ettarre; and upon the less luscious lips of any other person her meditative slow smile would have seemed unfeeling.

"Ah, well, but, in any event, I make no doubt that the Holy City has been modernized? and has been kept abreast, so to speak, with progress?"

"In Heaven there is no variableness nor any shadow of turning, as you should well know who used to be so fond of preaching from that text."

"Oh, my God!" said the good Bishop Odo, from force of habit: and the benevolence went out of his plump face.

For now contrition of the very sincerest sort had smitten him. He thought of his parishioners, of his misled lost flock, all decent, civilized, well-meaning communicants, entrapped, just by his over-fondness for rhetoric, into that fearful lair of multiheaded dragons and of all miscellaneous monstrosities. For these preposterous beasts, it seemed, were not mere figments of speech. There actually before him was one of the twelve pearls through which he had promised the flower of his little flock a glorious entry into Heaven: and the Book of the Revelation of St. John the Divine, in the teeth of all rational interpretation, was turning out to be something much worse than high-flown unintelligibility which you had to pretend to admire.

Inside that shining wall the hapless peasantry and the burghers whom his oratory had betrayed were now looked after by no benevolent bishop but were abandoned to the whims of unaccountable overlords, with hair like wool and with feet made of brass, who spent their time in blowing trumpets, and in opening vials full of plague germs, and in affixing sealing-wax to the foreheads of the defenceless dead. His little flock were now the appalled associates of huge locusts with human heads, and of wild horses with the tails of serpents, and of calves with eyes inset in their posterior parts. Nor were the perplexing customs and the patchwork animal-life of this barbaric bedlam atoned for by its climate, because every moment or two there was—so near as the Bishop could recall his sacred studies,—an earthquake or an uncommonly severe hailstorm: every moment or two the sun turned black, or the moon red, or else the stars came tumbling loose like fruit from a shaken fig tree; and seven thunders were intermittently conversing, for the most part about indelicate topics.

And Odo of Valnères, he also, who was so wholly dependent upon peaceful and refined surroundings, would presently be imprisoned in this awful place, for no real fault, but just through his well-meant endeavors to make life more orderly and more pleasant for his little flock. Already that infernal automatic cloud had moored itself.

10. OF HIS RIGHTEOUS ENDING ॐ

*I*NASMUCH as there seemed to be no alternative, the Bishop and the witch-woman disembarked, perforce, upon the bright wharf of Heaven. Now behind and below unhappy Odo of Valnères was only an endless gray abyss; beneath him showed great gleaming slabs like yellowish and bluish glass; and before him loomed inexorably the gate carved out of a giant pearl.

"Come, come!" a somewhat desperate prelate cried aloud, "but even now there must be some way of escape from that existence which I used to promise, in the days of my rash disbelief, as a reward?"

"There is," Ettarre replied to him, very proudly and happily; "for against love nothing can prevail. Why, but do you not understand! I am permitted to tempt you. Upon a cloud, of course, one feels a trifle insecure. But here we touch firm jasper and lapis lazuli. And now, with such allurements as you have not yet, I do believe, my wonderful enormous darling, quite utterly forgotten the way of, now I am going to preserve you from all sorts of celestial horrors."

"Eh, and is it possible, even at the last, for the welldoer to evade his doom? Is there some other and more suitable place yet open, upon post-mortem repentance, to a well-thought-of bishop?"

The dear child said then, still with that very touching fondness of which he felt himself to be unworthy:

"At the cost of just one tiny pleasant indiscretion, even

155

now, my own sweetheart, you will be refused admittance. You can then return with me to the more urbane and rationally conducted Paradise of the Pagans. And that is nothing like your so horrible and gaudy Kingdom of Heaven, but instead, it is a democracy which lacks for no modern improvements in the way of culture and of civilization."

Thereupon Ettarre began to speak as to her present abode in somewhat the opulent vein of an exceedingly young poet. And the good Bishop Odo, looking upon her with the old fondness, and with unforgotten delight in her dear loveliness, was aware of that in the large and curiously glittering eyes of Ettarre which, he was certain, nobody in that dreadful Oriental phantasmagoria just ahead could ever understand with quite that sympathy which moved in him rebelliously.

Ettarre, no doubt, was overcoloring some of her details. One exaggerated, for art's sake, in these descriptory passages. And he very well remembered how the little darling, when she was pretending to be a saint, had lied to him night after night with the unction of a funeral sermon. Even so, this adorable and cuddling witch-woman was a person whom Odo of Valnères, in his far-off pious youth, when he believed in saints, had cherished with a fervor and with a variousness not ever utterly to be put out of mind. And for the rest, the Bishop might, he felt just now—with all the sedative dilapidations of age thus marvelously repaired,—be happy enough, perhaps, in rewarding the warm loyalty of his Ettarre, among those cultured and broad-minded and intelligent circles which she described.

156

There remained only to allow for that slight girlish habit of unveracity.

Thus pensively did the Bishop begin to appraise the probabilities, in the while that from force of habit he made the sign of the cross, as he waited there, withholding his dark kindly eyes for a moment from the strangely large and glittering eyes of Ettarre, and looking downward, all through that rather lengthy moment in which he half paternally caressed the soft and the so lovely little hand of the dear love of his far-off, pious, hot-blooded youth; and she cuddled closer and yet closer to him and wriggled very deliciously in her candid and quite flattering affection.

At just this amiable season, the serenity of their re-union was overcast by the arrival of yet another cloud. It moored: and a child disembarked, a boy of seven or thereabouts, but newly dead and come alone through the gray void between Earth and Heaven. This little ghost passed by them as the child went uncertainly but meekly into the Holy City. The narrow shoulders were a trifle huddled, for these slabs of jasper and of lapis lazuli seemed more chilly to the small bare feet than had been the brown carpet of the child's nursery, and the soft arms of that mother whom he had left far behind him.

Now also Odo of Valnères had raised his very generally admired eyes from the neighborhood of his red flannel footwarmers, toward that huge and dazzling perforated pearl.

"I was thinking," he observed, with somewhat more of gentleness than of any plain connection, "that I

157

rather, as they put it, get on with children. My people
are so flattering as to say I have a way with them. I
could, I really do believe, have cheered that forlorn little
fellow tremendously with one of my simpler Confirma-
tion addresses, if we had travelled through that abyss
together. In fact, a clergyman of real talents, and of my
rather varied experience, could probably cheer up any
other saved soul in Heaven, in view of what must be the
local average of cheerfulness—"

"No doubt you could, my wonderful, kind-hearted,
clever darling," Ettarre replied. "But now that fearful
place, my precious, is a place with which you have no
further need to be bothering."

Odo of Valnères, however, was smiling with something of the enthusiast's fervor. Then, for one instant
only, he again looked downward, with the air of a man
as yet perplexed and irresolute, and again he crossed
himself, and he drew a deep breath which seemed to
inform him through and through with unpersuadable
determination.

Gently he put aside the love of his youth: and, with
that frank fine air of manliness which had always graced
his professional utterances, he spoke.

"No, sweetheart: for one of my cloth must not be
wholly selfish; and at a pinch a well-thought-of bishop
must choose for what seems to him a more noble and a
safer investment than is the happiness of which your
affection assures me. I had believed religion to be only
a narcotic and a restraint for man's misery upon earth.
I was wrong. I confess it, with humble contrition. And

my heart is aglow, Ettarre, with no ignoble fervor, to
discover that the profession to which I have devoted all
my modest abilities—such as they are, my dear,—must
always satisfy, for the better conducted of my fellow
beings, no merely temporal but an eternal requirement.
Even after death, I perceive, I am privileged to remain
the spiritual guide and consoler of my little flock—"

"But, my darling, the poor dears are already saved
beyond redemption; and so, to me, that sounds like nonsense."

"That is because you reason hastily, my pet. Yonder,
inside that shining wall, my people need me as never
before. More sorely now than in their mortal life they
require the feeling that some capable and tactful person mediates between them and the uncomfortably con-
tiguous contriver of their surroundings. Now, as not ever
in their merely earthly misery, they need the most eloquent assurances that these inconveniences are trivial
and by-and-by will prove transient. They need, in this
unsanitary, zoöplastic, explosive, and perturbing
Heaven, as they did not need in the more urbane at-
mosphere which I was always careful to maintain in my
diocese, to be sustained by salutary faith as to the oncoming rewards for prudent and respectable conduct.
So, you perceive, my dearest, I could not honorably
desert my little flock after having in some sense betrayed
them into their present condition. All these strong arguments are passing through my mind, my darling; and
they are reinforced by my firm conviction that the Ettarre whom I remember, both as a simple peasant girl

159

and as a blessed saint, did not use to have cloven feet like—shall I say?—a tender-eyed and very charming gazelle."

But now Ettarre, who during her most recent mortal life had been in practice among the witches of Amneran, as the most lovely of Satan's traps, had drawn a little away from Odo of Valnères in uncontrollable sorrow and disappointment.

"You have," she stated, "and you always did have, Odo, a mean and suspicious nature, quite apart from being a long-winded fat hypocrite. And you can talk from now to doomsday if you want to, but I think that to make a cross like that, when I was doing my very best for your real comfort, was cheating!"

"*Noblesse oblige*," replied the good Bishop Odo, with that impressiveness which he invariably reserved for any remark a trifle deficient in meaning. Then he went slowly but unfalteringly toward the gate marked "Levi."

Yet he looked back just once, through a mist of unshed, unepiscopal, and merely human tears, upon the grief of that delicious and so lovely Ettarre. Her distress over this final parting was becoming so passionate and extreme that it had turned the adorable child all black and scaly, and had set her to exhaling diversely colored flames. And Odo sighed to notice these deteriorations in her appearance, and in her deportment also, as his lost love assumed a regrettably dragonish shape, and with many frantic lashings of her tail swept whooping down the abyss.

After that, he removed his red flannel footwarmers,

as introductive of an undesirable chromatic note; he tidied his white nightgown into the general effect of a surplice; and the Bishop of Valnères went through that bright and lofty gate with appropriate dignity.

He was a bit surprised, though, when a tender voice said,—

"Welcome home, my Prettyman!"

Black Odo saw that the gates of this dubious, glaring place were now being locked, behind him, by dark, withered, and complacent looking, old Gui de Puysange.

Thus ends the history of that Odo called Le Noir, who nevertheless, even as the morning star makes light the womb of a black cloud, shone with the bright beams of his life and teaching; who by his radiance led into the light them that shivered in the gray cloud of the shadow of death; and who, like unto the rainbow giving light in the white clouds, set forth in his righteous ending the seal of his fond Master's covenant.

EXPLICIT